WAKULLA
SPRINGS

WAKULLA SPRINGS

ANDY DUNCAN

ELLEN KLAGES

Design and layout by Alligator Tree Graphics
Printed in England by T. J. International.

PS Publishing Ltd / Grosvenor House /
1 New Road / Hornsea, HU18 1PG / England

editor@pspublishing.co.uk / www.pspublishing.co.uk

STALKING THE ELUSIVE NOVELLA

ANDY DUNCAN & ELLEN KLAGES

*W*AKULLA *SPRINGS* IS A COLLABORATION THAT took almost twenty years. It began before the two of us had even met, and had long periods of dormancy, to say the least.

Sometime in the mid-1990s, Ellen was standing in the checkout line at her local grocery store, in San Francisco, leafing through an issue of the *National Enquirer*, when she happened on a large color photo of a chimp.

The chimp was dressed in a white shirt, suspenders, and old man pants. He was smoking a cigar and drinking whiskey. He was supposedly the chimp who had played Cheeta in the 1930s Tarzan movies, and was now sixty-something, the oldest chimp ever known. He was living in a trailer park in Los Angeles.

Ellen stopped and began to read, then added the tabloid to the milk and tea and popcorn in her shopping cart, and took it home.

She'd been a Tarzan fan since elementary school, when WBNS (in Columbus, Ohio) was the only channel that showed anything remotely interesting on Saturday afternoons: cartoons and old black-and-white movies, including Shirley Temple, the Marx Brothers, and the Johnny Weissmuller Tarzan series. (Her favorite was *Tarzan and the Amazons,* with Maria Ouspenskaya, and the forbidden city behind the impenetrable escarpment.)

The *Enquirer* article gave her a wisp of a fragment of an idea, so she cut it out and put it into a folder.

A year or so later—possibly two or three—she came across a *Reader's Digest* article about invasive species in Florida. Petting zoos and circuses let the animals go when the business went bankrupt. There were huge Burmese pythons, a population of several hundred monkeys along the Silver River, and flocks of wild parrots. When they made movies on location in the '30s, the crew would just release the animals when filming was complete, because one jungle seemed the same as another.

She put that article in the same folder with Cheeta. Over the next five years, the folder slowly filled with quasi-related articles, factoids, bits of information gleaned from Google, and other random flotsam that began to coalesce into a vaguely connected whole.

"There's a story here," she thought. "I wonder what it is?"

She discovered that many of the Tarzan movies had been filmed in Florida, some at the famous Silver Springs, and two at the previously unknown (to her) Wakulla Springs. "Wakulla" sounded mysterious, even sinister. She dug a little deeper and found the online resources of the Florida State Archives, which included photographs from the 1941 filming of *Tarzan's Secret Treasure.*

She was startled by pictures of local boys in blackface, dressed in loincloths. By men in safari hats urging an elephant off a dock. And fascinated by the world's deepest underwater spring, with underground tunnels so extensive they had never been fully explored.

Printouts went into the overflowing folder, which had branched out in many odd thematic directions.

In 2000 Ellen moved from San Francisco to Cleveland, to be near her elderly father and her sister Sally, who had Down Syndrome. Each March, she'd drive from Ohio to Florida for the International Conference on the Fantastic in the Arts (ICFA), starting out in frigid temperatures and snow, and gradually driving south into lush, verdant Spring on the way to Ft. Lauderdale.

In 2002, she made a stop in Tallahassee, the capital of Florida, and home to the state archive and library. (It turned out Tallahassee was nowhere near Ft. Lauderdale. It was almost 700 miles away. Florida was surprisingly big, and half the state was at right angles to the other half, with nothing but water as the hypotenuse.) Ellen spent an afternoon with piles and piles of folders full of newspaper clippings, photographs, and interviews with people involved with the Tarzan movies and Wakulla Springs.

A year later, her own folder was three inches thick, held together by rubber bands.

Late one night in early 2003, drinking wine and puzzling over how to turn all that information into an actual *story*, Ellen had an epiphany: *This is an Andy Duncan story. It's set in the deep South.*

Andy had a love of colorful talk, a sense of place, a yen for digression, a sense of humor, a fascination with the eccentric and quirky and grotesque, and an obsession with history and the supernatural in daily life. Everything in the folder spoke to that.

But she had no idea how Andy Duncan wrote a story. "He's brilliant," she thought. "I've read all his stories, and I still have no idea how he does it."

We were already admirers of each others' work, and had known each other socially for a few years, through science-fiction conventions, group dinners, and bar conversations. (Ellen was part of the makeshift choir that serenaded him with "The Andy Song" at the World Fantasy Convention in Montreal in 2001, when he won not one, but two awards for his fiction.)[1] And we were both at ICFA in March of 2003, in balmy, tropical Ft. Lauderdale, at a hotel that was slowly disintegrating into mildew.

Ellen found Andy around the pool, and said, "I have a story idea, let me pitch it to you and I'll get you a beer."

"I can't buy a story. I'm not editing an anthology or anything," Andy replied.

"I know." She gestured toward a table. "But I have this idea and I think it's an Andy Duncan story."

So she bought Andy a beer, and told him about Tarzan movies and wild monkeys and elderly chimpanzees and this odd springs near Tallahassee. Andy is a great listener, and a great talker, with an unmistakable Southern accent. He says, "I virtually spit grits whenever I open my mouth to speak." Very soon he began exclaiming, "Oh! Oh! What about *this*?"

There was another beer, and we both got really excited about the

---

1. "The Andy Song" was taught to the WFC choir for the occasion by Karen Joy Fowler, whose childhood next-door-neighbor, a boy named Andy, had created it as his own theme song. It goes something like this:

Who can climb the highest tree?

An—dy

Who can fight a bumblebee?

An–dy

Who can swim and who can dive?

Who's the greatest boy alive?

A-a-a-a-an-dy

What a guy is he!

various ideas and plots and characters and arcane bits of history that could be included.

Ellen offered to send him the folder and let Andy run with it. "I know there's a story in there somewhere," she said, "but I can't find the center of it. Since it feels like an Andy Duncan story, maybe you can."

Andy shook his head. "I think we should write it together. Maybe with both our names on it, we might even be able to sell it."

We lived a thousand miles from each other, and had busy lives, so we agreed to each think about what the story should be, and meet up the next year at ICFA to share the fruits of our labors. The next March, Ellen found Andy after a panel discussion and went over to him.

"Hey," she said.

"Hey. Thanks for all the research you xeroxed," he said. A long pause. "Have you done any work on that story?"

She shook her head. "I kept meaning to, but—"

"Oh, good!" he replied, and sighed in great relief. "I haven't either."

We looked at our schedules, found an open morning, and met on the porch of the poolside room Andy shared with his wife, Sydney. We sat in plastic chairs, drinking iced tea in the shade, and for two hours discussed characters and setting and plot. Uncharacteristically for either of us, we made an outline, so we'd have a fighting chance of being on the same page, and hammered out a four-act structure.

We agreed that we'd start with Andy writing the first draft of one chapter, with Ellen taking on the first draft of another. Once that was done, we'd figure out the other two bits. Excited and full of purpose, we went home to our respective desks, notebooks, and keyboards.

The next year, 2005, we met up at ICFA again.

Andy said, "What have you gotten done?"

Ellen said, slowly, with a hang-dog look, "Nothing."

"Oh, good, neither have I." And we went to the bar for a beer.

For five years, we met each March at ICFA, having lost no enthusiasm for the project, but having each written exactly nothing. We vowed again and again that by the *next* spring, there *would* be work in progress.

But each year, there was not.

So in 2010, by which time ICFA had moved to an airport Marriott in Orlando, Andy said, "You know what we have to do if we ever want to get this thing done? We need to hole up in a hotel, somewhere halfway between where you live and where I live, and just spend a week together knocking this sucker out."

Because Andy was teaching, summer was the only time we could meet. Andy had relocated to Frostburg, Maryland, and Ellen had moved back to San Francisco. We looked at a map, and halfway between those two places was—Oklahoma. Ellen refused to go to Oklahoma in the summer. She offered an alternate suggestion.

"What if we went to Tallahassee, to Wakulla Springs, where the movies were filmed?"

"That's brilliant," he said.

Although Andy had not written anything, he had done a lot of research, and found out that *Creature from the Black Lagoon* was also filmed at Wakulla Springs, twelve years after *Tarzan's Secret Treasure.*

As one might suspect by now, among other things, Andy and Ellen share a great love for research.

Andy: *I do entirely too much research, probably. Certainly from an economic standpoint, it doesn't make much sense to research a story as thoroughly as if it were a novel. But the research merely spurs the invention, gives me the courage to make things up. The best research advice I can give fiction writers is this: write down only the stuff that really inspires you, that gives you an idea for a character, an incident, a line of dialogue, a bit of cool description— something you can run with.*

Ellen: *I love research. It's so much easier than writing. Research is my time travel. Since I can't go back to the past and walk around, browse and shop and ask questions, I rely on contemporary sources—old magazines, objects from the '40s or '50s, photographs—and build up as much of that world as I can for myself. It's all about the details—what's different between the past and the present? What's the same? Once I can really* feel *the past—taste it, touch it, hear it, see it, smell it—I can try and recreate that on the page.*

~~~~~~~~~~

In June of 2010, we met up in Tallahassee, and got a two-bedroom suite, with a shared living room/kitchen, and rented a car. We planned to write 1,500 words a day, apiece.

Which we did not do.

We *did* drive the twenty miles down to Wakulla Springs (now a state park), where we took the boat tour and snapped photos, wandered through the old hotel, and interviewed people. Ellen had just gotten an iPad, so we had a GPS map. She drove and Andy had the tablet in his lap, giving directions and a running commentary about what was outside the windows. "Up on the left in about a hundred yards there's going to be a church—there's the church!"

We went to the county seat, Crawfordville, and visited the tiny historical society, located in a corner of the public library. We discovered archival references to Shadeville, the "colored" district near the springs, and looked at pictures of its school classes, making notes on hair styles and clothing, as Mayola and Levi began to materialize and accompany us on our walks.

Shadeville did not exist as an organized community by 2010, but we found where it had been, where the school had once stood. We followed dirt roads until they got too narrow for the rental car, then hiked around the backwoods of Florida's Panhandle. In June. It was 103 degrees, and 100 percent humidity. We drank a lot of water and took pages of damp notes. We discovered vine-and-creeper-clogged paths through the piney woods, got bitten by any number of savage bugs, found a sinkhole and an old graveyard. Then we went out and ate barbecue and drank beer and talked about what we'd seen, and how that might figure into the story.

At night, in the shared living room of the suite, we watched DVDs of Creature and Tarzan movies and talked to each other (it is a toss-up, who talks more, Ellen or Andy), and took more notes. We watched the opening of *Creature* over and over, borrowing from it for the introductory paragraph of the story.

That paragraph is the perhaps most truly collaborative bit in the novella, the only piece that we worked on together, in the same room, at the same time.

At one point, trying to figure out how to clue the reader in on the story's first historical timeframe—1941—we looked that year up in Wikipedia. We didn't want to baldly put 1941 at the top of the page, but since the story opens in June, and Pearl Harbor wouldn't happen for another six months, we needed another easily recognizable historical reference.

Wikipedia was not much help, although we did discover that F. Scott Fitzgerald and Nathanael West had died, a day apart, in December of 1940.

"I know. We can have someone walk into Gavin's store," Andy

drawled, "and proclaim: 'the golden age of literature is over. Nathanael West has died.'"

It might have been the late hour, or the beer, but this struck us both as so hysterically funny we almost fell off the couch laughing. We couldn't *use* it, obviously, and found another method of conveying the year, but the careful reader will notice that we did manage to sneak Nathanael West into another part of the story.

We are both enamored of the past. It's as if all times and places and people are co-existent, in some metaphorical but deeply meaningful and truthful way—historical figures are our next-door neighbors. We share their problems, so it's in our best interest to know something about them.

We spent one afternoon in the state library and archives (which was air-conditioned!) reading through boxes of original WPA interviews. Andy was over the moon, holding a sheaf of onionskin papers that Zora Neale Hurston herself had typed. We read about the local dialect of the times, about geography and history. We took copious, careful notes about the ugly realities fostered by Jim Crow laws and segregation in every aspect of life.

At the end of a very full week, during which Andy had managed to write perhaps 600 words, and Ellen about the same, we left Tallahassee. At the airport, we each promised to sit down the minute we got home and write our complete drafts. "I'll email you 5000 words by the end of next week," Ellen said.

She didn't.

Neither did he.

We *did* do more research.

In the tangle of material Ellen had collected, Andy was especially intrigued by the exotic-animal thread. Wakulla Springs was a locale where remarkable real-life fossils had been unearthed and it was a filmmaking location for one of the most celebrated monster movies of the 1950s, a movie inspired by a folktale of beasts unknown to science.

At a dinner party during the filming of *Citizen Kane*, actor William Alland heard Mexican cinematographer Gabriel Figueroa pass on the tall tale of a race of human/fish hybrids that supposedly lived in the Amazon. Andy wondered whether such a tradition actually existed in the Amazon, or whether Figueroa was just pulling Alland's leg. Because, when Alland became a movie producer for Universal-International ten years later, he turned elements of Figueroa's yarn into *Creature from the Black Lagoon*.

Andy delved deep into accounts of the remarkable second-unit underwater footage for *Creature*, filmed at Wakulla Springs, including an unforgettable erotic *pas de deux* between an unsuspecting beauty swimming above and a curious beast shadowing her movements below. The two swimmers onscreen were really two young veterans of Florida's gloriously kitschy Weeki Wachee mermaid show: Ricou Browning, in the Gill-Man suit, and Ginger Stanley, the stand-in for leading lady Julia Adams. Just as Stanley doubled Adams onscreen, so the Wakulla River doubled for the Amazon in all the boat-shot footage of junglelike flora passing in the background.

Creature provides a vaguely scientific rationale for the Gill-Man (whose gender never is in doubt, not for one moment, in the movie): He's a living fossil, the alive-and-well modern version of the prehistoric creature exhumed in the opening sequence by Dr. Maia, played by former silent-film star Antonio Moreno. Though Dr. Maia is oblivious to the webbed and clawed hand that reaches from the water, it is an exact duplicate of the (remarkably well-preserved) fossilized hand he's holding. Dating the hand from the Devonian Era, Dr. Maia calls his find "very important"—and well he might, since the only Devonian land creatures known to actual science were a lot more primitive than the bipedal, humanoid Gill-Man.

Andy discovered that the movie's instantly iconic monster, a triumph not of biology but of Hollywood arts and sciences, was largely the design of the brilliant Milicent Patrick, subject of a fascinating 2011 *Tor.com* article by Vincent Di Fate. (That neither Ellen or Andy managed to work in at least one scene featuring a fictionalized version of Ms. Patrick remained one of Andy's few regrets about the project. Another is that we also ignored Ginger Stanley, though she was right there at the springs with Browning, and certainly could have interacted with Levi during that chapter of the novella.)

What made all this *Creature* lore as personal to Andy as Tarzan was to Ellen was his lifelong fascination with cryptozoology, the pseudoscientific search for large animals believed by mainstream science to be extinct or imaginary. As a twelve-year-old, Andy avidly read every book he could find at the Batesburg-Leesville public library about the Loch Ness Monster, Bigfoot, the Abominable Snowman, Thunderbirds, man-eating trees, the whole menagerie, never dreaming all this might be helpful to his career one day. He now regards cryptozoology as less a science than a mishmash of dubious anecdotes, logical fallacies, outright hoaxes, and relentlessly literal-minded misappropriations of indigenous belief.

But he can't stop reading about it, either, because it's all grist for the mill, and because, frankly, he's more in touch with his inner twelve-year-old than most middle-aged people care to be, except perhaps, Ellen, which is one of the qualities that drew us together to begin with.

The traditional stories of weird critters in the woods or the rivers or the swamps, told in every locality—the beliefs that long predate the homogenized, generic Bigfoots, chupacabras, and Mothmen of contemporary pop culture—continued to fascinate Andy, and from the outset of the *Wakulla Springs* project, he was determined to drop into the manuscript the names of every Florida-specific cryptid he could find.

Fast forward eighteen months after that trip to Tallahassee.

By the fall of 2011, oddly enough, we'd both finally managed to get words down on paper. Ellen had written the first draft of one chapter, while Andy wrote a draft of another. We swapped text files over email.

Then Andy sent Ellen a very long draft. She edited it and fiddled with it, changing some of the dialogue, adding bits of exposition, moving some sections around, and sent it back after a week or two. By then school was back in session and Andy was teaching. Ellen didn't expect to hear from him immediately, and the e-mail said, "I know you're busy, and the semester's just started, but let me know that you got this. You don't have to *do* anything, just let me know."

After about a month, she still hadn't heard from him. She sent him another email, reassuring him that she didn't expect him to be *working* on it much during the semester, but to please let her know that he'd received the file.

Another month. Another email: *Just let me know you've gotten it.*

No response. Ellen thought, "Oh God, we hadn't talked about this part of the collaborative process. Maybe Andy's not used to being edited? Maybe he's really offended by the changes I made?"

Silence. A month later, she even sent an e-mail to his wife, Sydney, saying, "Could you ask Andy to check his e-mail?"

Nothing.

In March of 2012, we were both at ICFA. It had been almost six months since Ellen sent Andy the edited file, and there had been no communication between us. On the first day of the conference,

Ellen walked into the coffee shop, and Andy waved, then stood up and gave her a big hug. Neither mentioned the story.

But an hour later, when we were standing by the registration desk, Ellen got up the courage to ask, "Are you mad at me?"

Andy stared down at her. (Andy is close to six feet tall; Ellen is a hair over five feet.) "No, why?"

"Because I sent you a big edited file six months ago, and I never heard back from you."

Andy hung his head. "I am so bad."

"What?"

"I am *so* bad."

She raised an eyebrow.

"Well," he continued. "I was teaching, and I had a new collection coming out, and I was kinda swamped. And after a while I felt embarrassed that I hadn't answered any of your emails, and then it got to be *such* a long time that—" He let the sentence drift off across the lobby.

Ellen nodded. "But you're not mad?"

He said "No, no. Those were all really good changes."

All was well, and we went to the bar and discussed the existing text at great length, and figured out what still needed to be written, and which of us should give it a try.

The story continued to grow. And grow.

By the summer of 2012, nearly ten years after our first chimp-and-jungle conversation, all the parts were written, and just needed a bit of polish and editing, a few adjustments—and a title.

We were both at Readercon, outside Boston, in mid-July, and over yet another round of beers, we sat in the hotel bar and talked about the finished draft. Andy said, "Do you think we should put something fantastic in here? There's nothing fantastic. I mean it's *about* Tarzan, and it's *about* the Creature from the Black Lagoon, and that's about as fantastical and science fictional as it gets. But—"

"Yeah, I know." Ellen thought about that for a minute. It was not the first time we'd asked each other the same question. "What do you want to do?"

Andy shrugged. "I really like it the way it is, but I'm afraid we're never gonna sell it to any of the magazines that publish us."

We decided not to change it. We were really happy with it as it was. We did toss around a few prose-fixes, made some last-minute adjustments. Then we sat around and talked about the title for more than an hour, scribbling possibilities onto cocktail napkins. We wanted to call it something reasonably short that would encompass all of the various themes and ideas in the story, and kept failing to find anything that even remotely worked.

Part of the problem was that each of us had been referring to the story differently all along. To Andy, the Sunshine State—just like the South Carolina peach orchards, pecan groves and piney woods where he grew up—was a fantasyland long before Walt Disney bought up 30,000 acres of wetlands and orange groves a half-century ago. During the decade that we worked on the novella, although Ellen always referred to it as "the Tarzan story," for Andy, it was always "the Florida story."

Alas, neither of those worked as a title.

In the end, Ellen remembers that it was Sydney, who had joined us in the bar, late in the process, who said, "You all are making it too complicated. What's wrong with just *Wakulla Springs*?"

Not a thing. And so it became.

Andy had given Ellen the onerous honor of the last edit, because this had all been her idea, originally. She spent about a month turning her syntax into Andy Duncan-ish sentence structure, and vice versa. (It turned out that while he was writing, he was thinking:

What would Ellen do here? And she was similarly pondering: *How would this sound if Andy was reading it aloud?*)

Ultimately, our styles are similar enough that by the end of the final edit, even we had trouble remembering, line by line, who had written what, exactly.

Our goal had been to declare the work *done* before Christmas of 2012, and we made it with days to spare. We'd debated where to submit this very odd, very long story, and chose *Tor.com* as its initial destination.

We looked up their submission requirements, which were something like: *Absolutely nothing over 17,500 words unless you've won the Nobel Prize.* The finished novella was around 35,000 words.

Hmm.

We sent a query email to editor Patrick Nielsen Hayden, saying, "We really *have* looked at your submission requirements and we do know that this is more than twice as long as anything you're willing to accept, but would you like to see it anyway?"

Patrick wrote back and said something along the lines of, "You and Andy Duncan? That's intriguing. I'll take a look at it."

Scuttlebutt had it that *Tor.com* took anywhere between six weeks and six months to respond to submissions. But around the middle of January of 2013, Andy sent off an e-mail to Patrick saying, "Hey, it's been three weeks, and we were just wondering if you've had a chance to look at *Wakulla Springs.*"

"I'm reading it now," Patrick replied by return email. He bought it the next day, and said there'd be an editorial letter coming in a week or two.

Andy and Ellen exchanged nervous emails. How much would he want us to change? How much were we *willing* to change? In the end, Patrick asked us to rewrite two sentences and replace a single, slightly anachronistic, word in another. That was it for alterations to our 130-page manuscript.

Huge sighs of relief.

Wakulla Springs was published online at *Tor.com* on October 2, 2013, with a beautiful illustration by Gary Kelley.

Reception was mostly complimentary. "Uniquely American magic realism." "Beautifully written." But there were a few rumblings about the story being an invasive species in the genre world.

"Can someone clarify for me why this was published by Tor? Outside the authors' track records, and one scene, there was *nothing* SFnal about this."

2013 turned to 2014, and awards season began. *Wakulla Springs* made several best-of-the-year lists. Its inclusion was praised on dozens of blogs and denounced on as many others. Not SF. Not fantasy. Not genre.

We were thrilled when it received a Nebula nomination, and over the moon when it was also nominated for a Hugo. That seemed to gall a lot of fans online, who posted repeatedly that it did not qualify. "It would be my number-one pick, but I cannot vote for a story that isn't SF." The lack of the overtly fantastic offended many genre purists.

As the year progressed, the novella was also nominated for the Locus Award and the World Fantasy Award. Neither Andy nor Ellen had ever done a hat-trick—had a story nominated for *all* the major awards in our field. We'd never written anything before that got that kind of attention.

In November it won the World Fantasy Award for best novella. It was Ellen's first Lovecraft bust (the coveted, but controversial "big ugly head") and Andy's third.

Is the story science fiction? Perhaps not.

Is it fantasy? Perhaps not.

But is it SFnal? Yes.

It came out of a deep lifelong love for the genre of the fantastic that both of us shared. Besides, the story absolutely depends on the reader's knowledge of the history of fantasy and science fiction in the twentieth century.

We stand upon the shoulders of giants.

Tarzan is one of the best known fictional characters in the world. Ray Bradbury (a hero and inspiration for both of us) once said that Edgar Rice Burroughs was probably the most influential fantasy writer in history, because his work is so ubiquitous, and Tarzan is such a cultural icon.

And where would science fiction be without monsters? (Frankenstein, anyone?) Mid-twentieth-century, post-war science-fiction culture boasts more than 500 monster movies. Imaginary beasts, strange and terrifying mysteries. Granted, the most obvious monsters in our story are those who use laws, not claws, but that cryptozoological beings seem to make a cameo appearance at the end of the story is quite obviously a shout-out to the Gill-Man and his brethren. Some readers have misread the *woomp, woomp* and the clutching hand as the story's only speculative elements, and theorized that the authors inserted them as a last-minute sop to the SFnal-minded editors of *Tor.com*, allowing them to justify publishing the story in the first place.

In fact, that last page is there to reinforce the promise set out in the opening paragraph, to bring the story full circle:

Wakulla Springs. A strange and unknown world, this secret treasure lies hidden in the jungle of northern Florida. In its unfathomable depths, a variety of curious creatures have left a record of their coming, of their struggle to survive, and of their eventual end. Twenty-five thousand years after they disappeared from the face of the Earth, the bones of prehistoric mastodons, giant armadillos, and other primeval monsters have been found beneath the seemingly placid surface of the lagoon. The visitor to this magical place enters a timeless world of mystery.

Wakulla Springs is the story of a Florida family across three generations. It is also the story of a creature-haunted, legend-forged, tall-tale landscape that is no less fantastical for being accurate in its every detail. If you don't believe that, check into a hotel in Tallahassee—or, better yet, into the Wakulla Springs Lodge itself—and spend a week exploring the environs, as Andy and Ellen did on a fateful working vacation years ago.

A NOTE ABOUT THIS EDITION

Wakulla Springs was published online in 2013. For the first two years of its existence, there was no print edition. We had written this novel-like-thing that had no corporeal reality.

Then it was translated for *Science Fiction World*, China's largest SF magazine, in the February 2015 issue. There it was, typeset and on paper, but neither of us read Chinese. We did discover that the Tarzan yell (*Aaahhh-eeeeeeee-aaahhhh-eeeee-aaaahhhh-eeeeee-aaaahhhhh!* in our version) is just as easily recognizable in non-English characters.

Later in 2015, as a promotional giveaway at the World Fantasy Convention in Saratoga Springs, *Tor.com* produced two very limited edition "stubby" hardcovers (approx. 4 x 6 inches), choosing Kai Ashante Wilson's novelette, *The Devil in America,* and our novella, *Wakulla Springs* (with the Kelley illustration as its cover), to showcase this unique format. Those books were never officially offered for sale, though secondhand copies occasionally change hands.

We are grateful to Peter and Nicky Crowther and PS Publishing for reprinting our story in this beautiful edition, giving it a new audience, and giving us a tangible, physical object to add to our bookcases.

WAKULLA
SPRINGS

Wakulla Springs. A strange and unknown world, this secret treasure lies hidden in the jungle of northern Florida. In its unfathomable depths, a variety of curious creatures have left a record of their coming, of their struggle to survive, and of their eventual end. Twenty-five thousand years after they disappeared from the face of the Earth, the bones of prehistoric mastodons, giant armadillos, and other primeval monsters have been found beneath the seemingly placid surface of the lagoon. The visitor to this magical place enters a timeless world of mystery.

1

SECRET
TREASURE

"WELL, THERE YOU IS, MAYOLA." VERGIE JACKSON looked up from the porch of the shotgun cabin on the edge of the piney woods, waving a paper fan with a faded picture of Jesus. "I like to die in this heat, a-waiting."

"I told you," Mayola Williams said. "I was helping Miz Green close up the school for the summer."

"You said you'd be home 'bout noon. It's near two o'clock."

Mayola shrugged. "We got to talking, and I lost track of the time." She shifted a stack of books from one hip to the other. "Lemme set these in the house and we can go someplace cooler. I won't be a minute."

"What for she give you homework in the *summer*?"

"Ain't homework. Just some books she loaned me to read."

"What kind?"

"The kind they teach up at the A&M."

Vergie rolled her eyes. "I want to be quit of school, and you always asking for more. I don't see the point of it."

"Well. How 'bout this?" Mayola took the top book off the stack and held it up, just out of Vergie's reach.

"They Eyes Was Watching God," Vergie sounded out slowly. "That's just Bible study."

"Nope. It's a story novel."

Vergie fanned herself again. "Make believe." She shook her head.

"But look here." Mayola showed the back cover. "Wrote by a real-life colored woman. She from Florida, too." She laid the book on top of the others with gentle care, then went into the house, the rickety screen door slapping shut behind her.

She reappeared a few minutes later. "Let's go over to Cherokee Sink. I'm all over sweaty, and a swim would sure feel good." Mayola liked to swim about as much as anything, except to read, and it'd been nearly a week since she'd been able to kick loose all the kinks and sitting aches.

"Uh-uh. My brothers gone over there, and Luke Callen's with 'em. That boy's mean as a sack a'snakes."

"True enough. How 'bout the river then? Lower Bridge only ten minutes more."

"I can't swim nowheres this week. I got my monthlies."

"Oh." There was no arguing with that. Mayola thought for a minute. "Tell you what. Miz Green give me twelve cents for helping her clean. I put it all in my piggy bank, 'cept for one Indian head penny—that's good luck, and I put it right into my shoe, so it'll watch out for me. But I reckon I could spare a nickel to walk over to Gavin's store and get us an RC Cola from the ice chest. That's almost as cool as swimming."

"Let's get us some goobers, too." Vergie pulled on a pair of laceless, formerly white Keds.

"I don't know. That's another nickel."

"And you saving up for college. I know. I know. I been hearing 'bout your biggity dream ever since Miz Green put that bug in your ear. But this's *my* treat." Vergie paused, to make sure Mayola was paying her proper attention. "I got me a whole quarter."

"How?" Vergie never did a lick of work if there was some way round it.

"Odell Watkins. He kinda sweet on me, and he got hisself a job up at the springs, rowing white folks out on the river. He shows 'em a sleeping gator and some old bones way deep under the water, and they *tip*." She held up the coin with a satisfied smile.

Mayola didn't think much of Odell, but a cold soda was nothing to fuss about, so she just nodded, and they headed down the sandy track out to the Shadeville Road. She was a tall, slender girl with long muscular legs. Vergie was a head shorter and sashayed as she walked, all hips and curves. The soles of her Keds were coming unglued, and made a flap-scritch-flap sound when they hit the gravel.

"I need to get me a pair of shoes somebody else ain't worn out first."

"You could save up Odell's quarter."

"What for? We thirsty *today*," Vergie said.

The sides of the road were shallow, weed-filled ditches, jumping with grasshoppers and chigger bugs, and there was nary a car, so they walked down the center. By the time they'd gone a few hundred yards in the fierce June sun, Mayola could feel the thin cotton of her dress sticking to her back, damp as if she was laundering it from the inside-out.

The one-room white-washed store sat at the crossroads, its tin roof and bright red Coca-Cola sign glinting in the sun. Inside it was dark and cool and smelled of briny pickles and sweet Moon Pies. A man in bib overalls stood by the counter, talking louder than polite conversation called for.

"You think just 'cause Roosevelt's in for the third time, we gonna get the electric down here? May as well wish in one hand and spit in the other." He threw a sack of potatoes over his shoulder with a grunt. "Sometime I think you tetched in the head, Frank Gavin."

The storekeeper watched him go, then turned to Vergie. "What can I do *you* for, young lady?"

"Two RCs and a pack of salt peanuts," she said, laying her quarter down on the rough counter. She got a mercury dime in change, Mayola noticed. That was lucky, too.

Mayola set the peanuts on the windowsill, cellophane crinkling and sticking to her sweaty palm, before she plunged her whole arm into the galvanized ice chest by the door. Her hand closed around the soda bottle right away, but she held it there long enough for her skin to remember what cold was. When Vergie made a my-turn sound, she pulled it out and popped the bottle cap with the church key that hung on twine by the door.

Outside, they sat in the shade of the roof overhang, on a crate stenciled MOBILGAS. Mayola wrapped her hand around the top of her bottle, making a funnel, and Vergie poured in half the bag of peanuts. One by one they fizzed bubbles as they sank, then the bottle was all a-foam, peanuts floating back up in a sweet, salty slurry. That first sip was just about close to heaven.

"Odell's taking me to a dance next Friday night," Vergie said when her soda was most gone.

Mayola was finishing off her peanuts, tilting the bottle and tapping on the bottom to get the very last one, so it was a minute before she could reply. "Where 'bouts?" News of a dance went around pretty quickly in their small town, but she hadn't heard a peep.

"Cooper's." Vergie let the word hang out in the air.

"Vergie Jackson!" Mayola dropped her bottle right onto the ground. "Cooper's nothing but a jook joint."

"I know." Now she was smiling like the cat that ate the canary.

"But you took the pledge in Sunday school, same as me," Mayola said, and heard the prissy in her own voice.

"Just 'cause I'm gonna dance, don't mean I got to drink."

But she would, Mayola thought. Vergie'd been edging toward wildness and forbidden fruit ever since she started her turn from child to woman. "Your daddy's gonna have a conniption, he hears you was anywhere near that place." She shivered, even in the heat. Reverend Jackson was hellfire on sinners.

"He ain't gonna hear nothing. I'll tell him I'se staying over at your place. And I will. But not til pretty late. If I leave my church dress with you, come Sunday morning, I can walk in shiny bright and full'a the spirit, a-men."

"You asking me or telling me?" Mayola crossed her arms over her chest and tried to look fearsome.

"You my friend?"

"Yeah. But, Vergie. A jook joint's mighty—"

"I'm going." Vergie held up her hand. She stood up, and *did* look fearsome. Then she smiled, sweet as spun sugar, and just as full of air. "C'mon. Do me this itty bitty favor, and I reckon I can do you a big one right back."

"I don't need no favor." Mayola picked up her soda bottle and put it in the crate for the RC man to take back.

"Oh yeah? How'd you like to add to that piggy bank? Three dollars a week."

"Three *dollars*?" That was near as much as her brother Charles was making, cutting pulpwood for St. Joe. Hard work. She narrowed her eyes and stared at Vergie. "You got yourself into some mischief?"

Vergie shook her head. "Ain't got nothing to do with me. Odell say they looking for girls to work in the Lodge up at the springs."

"Doing what?"

"Kitchen work. Cleaning rooms. Maybe some waitressing too. I don't know 'bout that, though. White folks don't care much who make their food, but seems they real particular 'bout who puts it on the table."

"Three dollars a week? You sure?" Mayola was quick-like doing the numbers in her head. School didn't start up again until mid-September. Three months was twelve weeks was—thirty-six dollars! That would more than triple up her piggy bank, and she'd been saving on that for better than a year.

"We can find out easy enough." Vergie pointed to the woods that ran behind the store. "We take the logging road, it's only a couple three miles to the springs, and it's most all shade."

Mayola sat still for a tiny little moment. She liked to think on a thing, make a plan, before she set off to do it. Not like Vergie. But if they were hiring up at the springs, and word got round, those jobs would be gone fast as cornbread off a hungry man's plate. It couldn't hurt to ask. She nodded once, and they headed east, toward the trees.

Most girls who grew up in Shadeville knew the piney woods as well as they knew their own kitchens—the snakey places to watch out for, the shortcuts, the swimming holes and sinks, the back ways into everywhere. So it was a only matter of minutes before Vergie stopped at a narrow break in the dense green wall, and they stepped off the wiry grass and disappeared from view.

The path was so narrow they had to go single file, brushing away the creeper vines and scrub branches that threatened to choke off what trail there was. Insects droned and buzzed and clicked all around them, like a thousand tiny New Year's noisemakers. The sun was only a memory above the impenetrable canopy, but the air felt thick and close, like it was considering changing its name to steam.

Vergie slapped at her arm, then her leg, and after the third slap, untied the kerchief from her neck and wrapped it around her head.

"That gonna help?" Mayola asked.

"Maybe. Mama used some new kind of hair oil when she ironed me out this week, and I think the skeeters like it." She knotted the kerchief at the back. "Got perfume smells like flowers, I guess."

The path ended at a long, wide slash running north through the tangle, broad enough for a wagon. Down the middle, a dusty-green brush of grass and weeds divided the sand as far ahead as they could see, flanked by traces of wheel ruts.

Now the going was easier, and they walked side-by-side, pine needles and a scatter of dry leaves underfoot, birds calling unseen from the trees. *Chee-chee-chee. Yip-yip-yip-yip-yip. Heee-ee. Heee-ee.* Twisted scrub oaks and longleaf pines lined the road, the pine trunks as straight and bare as pencils, the wide leaves of the oaks not quite meshing overhead, so the ground was dappled with a calico of sun and shade. Once or twice Mayola felt a breeze run down the corridor, whispering leaves against each other and cooling her almost to the edge of comfort.

"Hold up," she said after they'd been walking in silent company for fifteen minutes. "I'm gonna get some gum. Want a piece?"

"That'd be fine."

Mayola stepped over roots and low brush, avoiding the bright green trios of poison ivy, and entered a clearing a few yards in. The bark of the pines had been slashed, revealing raw yellow wood, glistening with beads of resin. Narrow strips of tin formed shallow V-shaped troughs stacked one of top of the other, a few inches apart, like an angular column of Cheshire cats. Nothing but smiles.

It was an old gum patch, where woodriders like her father used to bleed the pines for the turpentine stills. Mayola stopped at a tree as big around as her waist. A clay pot, its edges glittering with dried sap, hung at eye level. She pinched a wad of sticky amber resin from the cut above the pot and rolled it across her palm until it was the size of a store-bought gumball. She popped it in her mouth, savoring the clean pine taste between her teeth, then made a second one for Vergie.

The back of her neck prickled, and she felt something that was not Vergie watching her. She looked around. Up there in the shady darkness among the tree branches, a thing with small black eyes looked down on her. Probably just a possum. But it didn't look quite like a possum's face, and didn't that paw look more like a hand? Mayola felt with her toes to make sure her penny was still where it ought to be, and walked fast out of the gum patch.

They stayed on the path another twenty minutes, the whole world as narrow as a tunnel, with green straight up and down on the sides and white sand straight ahead. Then a dark and horizontal line appeared, a quarter mile in front of them. The county road. An old black truck rumbled into view and was gone again two seconds later.

"Almost there," Vergie said. She took off her kerchief and stuffed it into her pocket.

"Pretty near." Mayola felt her stomach tumble over inside. Not scared, really. Just wondering what was going to happen. By the time they reached the road, she'd made sure all her buttons were done up and her collar was straight, and tugged at her dress, pulling it so the fabric unwrinkled a bit and a puff of air cooled the damp at the small of her back.

The road was two lanes, paved flat. The trees fell back behind ditches, and she could see the sky again, a pale, cloudless blue. She looked both ways then crossed over, the tar hot even through the soles of her shoes. Ten yards to the left was the back road into Wakulla Springs.

The springs had been there for years—millions, according to Mr. Monroe, the science teacher. He said that hairy elephants and camels and armadillos the size of Chevys had once lived around here. Mayola thought those animals being real was about as likely as the tales her brothers told about ghosts and swamp varmints that ate up people who wandered where they shouldn't. But her grandaddy said he'd swum in the springs when he was a boy, so they were for sure old.

The buildings weren't. She'd been in the fifth grade when her uncles got work digging up land and nailing boards and pouring cement for Mr. Ball's hotel. Most everybody in the county worked for Mr. Ball, one way or another. He ran the paper company and the mill and—

Vergie let out a long, low whistle. "Holy Joe!" She pointed to a line of black cars—new cars—polished like mirrors so the shine like to blind a person in the hot sun.

"Rich people," Mayola said in a whisper. No wonder the pay was three dollars a week.

"Ain't that many rich people in the whole county."

"Maybe Mr. Ball got visitors from Tallahassee. He know a lot of business folk, even senators, I suppose. They all rich."

The road led to a courtyard at the front of the Lodge, with its gleaming white walls and red tile roof. The parking area was full of more cars than Mayola had ever seen in one place before. At the far end, nosed every which way, were a dozen or more trucks— pickups and flatbeds for hauling, and one closed off all the way around, with bars on the sides like a box of animal cookies.

Both girls stopped, out of sight behind a massive oak tree, and stared, their mouths open. "Something *big* is going on here," Vergie said, and the excitement in her voice matched what Mayola was feeling at the same exact moment.

Nothing big ever happened in Wakulla County.

She was just catching her breath again and readying herself to go find out about what they'd come for, when they heard a screech of grinding metal that like to cut the air in two. She watched as a white man in a strap undershirt pushed up the back of the cage truck, pulled down a ramp, and poked inside with a long hooked stick.

Mayola almost swallowed her gum when, slow as a Sunday stroll, a for-real elephant walked out into the Florida sun.

"Aaahhh-eeeeeeee-aaahhhh-eeeee-aaaahhhh-eeeeee-aaaah-hhhh!"

A long, ululating cry pierced the quiet of the jungle.

"That's Tarzan!" Boy said. "He's going for a swim!" Boy grabbed Cheeta's paw and they raced through the wiry grass until they came to the bank of the mighty river. A fallen tree lay across a branch of a taller tree, overhanging the water. As nimbly as any young ape, Boy scampered up the steep angle to stand beside his father, leaving Cheeta below to watch.

Tarzan stood high above the slow-moving river, naked except for a triangular loincloth low on his hips, his knife sheathed at his side. He was a magnificent man, his thick hair long and dark, his skin the color of honey. He was poised and ready to dive, every inch of his smoothly muscled body as sleek and lithe as an animal's, showing at a glance his wondrous combination of enormous strength, suppleness, and speed. His deep, brooding eyes scanned his realm.

The ape-man might be ignorant of the ways of civilization, uneducated, childlike in his puzzlement about the tools of the white man. But this was *his* world, and in it, he was the most cunning, the most intelligent, the most respected—and most feared—of all the creatures. King of the Jungle.

"Umgawa!" he said to Boy. And without another word—for he was a man of few words—Tarzan took another step out onto the limb, flexed his powerful legs and—

"Cut!" yelled the director.

Johnny Weissmuller relaxed. He looked down into the crystal clear waters of Wakulla Springs for a moment, then cuffed little Johnny Sheffield on the shoulder, and the two actors climbed down the ladder hidden from the cameras on the far side of the tree. On the ground, his assistant helped him into his white terrycloth robe, its edges stained brown from his full-body makeup. Weissmuller was as tan as any man in Hollywood, but Tarzan had to be flawless.

"Boy go for swim?" he asked.

Sheffield shook his head. "I've got to do my schoolwork. Union rules."

"Swim tomorrow," Weissmuller said, and ruffled his blond curls.

A colored boy rowed them across the water to the movie encampment with its folding canvas chairs, tents, and trunks of equipment. Weissmuller slouched into the chair stenciled BIG JOHN, and watched as Little John ran across the manicured lawn and into the Lodge for his lessons.

Cameras were mounted on a floating barge in the middle of the river. Beyond them, two stunt doubles now stood on the tree branch, and at a signal from Thorpe, the director, they dived head-first into the deep, clear water. One of them faltered and made a huge splash.

"Crap!" said Thorpe. He turned to the swimming coordinator. "We have to shoot that again, Newt. Tarzan doesn't *splash*, for crissakes."

"Can do." Newt Perry waited for the two Tallahassee lifeguards to swim over to the platform. "He wants it again. Make it a clean entry, this time."

The smaller of the two boys grinned. "At fifty bucks a dive, I'll go in any way he wants."

"Just dry off and get back up there. The sun's almost below the trees."

Johnny watched from his chair. Even with the canvas umbrella, he could feel the heat of the sun on his back. Time for a cold one. He waited for the cameras to roll again and watched as two men carried a big wooden crate around the side of the hotel, struggling to keep it upright.

With a grunt, they lowered it to the ground next to a big wire cage outside the prop tent. Weissmuller could hear angry screeches from inside the box.

"What's in there?"

"Monkeys." The man opened the cage door and jerked a thumb over his shoulder. "Two more crates up there. Turtles and some kinda birds. Parrots, I think."

He pulled on a pair of heavy gloves while his partner used a crowbar to open the lid, splintering it. The gloved man grabbed the nimble little animals by the scruffs of their necks as they clambered out, and tossed them into the cage.

"How're you going to ship them back?" Weissmuller pointed to the ruined crate.

"Don't have to. One jungle's the same as another. We'll just let 'em go when the shoot's over." He closed the cage, rattled the handle to make sure it was latched, and headed back toward the hotel.

"Quiet on the set!" the assistant director yelled through his megaphone.

Johnny turned back to the action above the river.

The next dive was as slick as a whistle, almost as good as he could have done himself. He flexed his shoulders. He hated the idea of a stunt double, but the studio demanded it. At two grand a week, he was too valuable to risk. He glanced at the thirty-foot diving platform over the deepest part of the springs. Thorpe had been away yesterday afternoon for a meeting, and Johnny had spent an hour diving off again and again, happy as a kid. The other guests at the Lodge had gathered around, applauding.

That was okay, too.

"We almost done?" he called to the assistant director after he'd yelled *Cut!*

"Yeah. Losing the light." The man walked over, looking at his watch. "I should remind Thorpe he's got dinner with Mr. Ball in an hour. Coat and tie for the dining room."

And a direct line of sight across the lawn to the platform. No diving tonight. "Okay." Weissmuller stood up, towering over the other man. "I'm going to change, drive into town."

"Thorpe says—" He paused. "—He says to keep it in your pants and go easy on the booze. You've got close-ups tomorrow. Ten o'clock call."

Johnny shrugged. "Tarzan have fun." It wasn't his idea to film in a dry county. He stepped over the tangle of cables and headed for his room in the Lodge. His robe open, his feet bare, he padded quietly across the terrazzo floor of the lobby, almost as silently as if he *were* the king of this jungle.

Twenty minutes later, showered and shaved, his long hair slicked back and tamed with Brylcreem, he stepped out of the elevator and looked around the ornately tiled lobby. He'd been told the hand-painted designs on the cypress beams of the ceiling were Moorish, with a little art-deco Mayan, like Grauman's, but they reminded him of the barns in the Pennsylvania Dutch country where he grew up.

He smiled and strode down the hallway to the front door. It would have seemed unlikely to any observer that the man in the crisp, short-sleeved tropical weight shirt and knife-creased linen slacks had been swinging half-naked through the primeval forest an hour before.

"Black Packard," he said, tossing the keys to a colored boy.

"Yessuh." He brought the convertible around, chrome winking golden in the last of the afternoon sun, and held the door open.

Johnny Weissmuller nodded his thanks, flipped the boy a coin, and got behind the wheel. He slid his sunglasses from under the visor, put them on, and angled the sleek car out on to the highway that led north to Tallahassee. Twenty miles between him and the admiring young co-eds of the Florida State College for Women. A good night to be a movie star.

———————

The Wakulla Springs Lodge was a palace, out in the middle of nowhere, a private country club surrounded on all sides by gator-filled swamps and piney woods. It was only a few years old, and had been built to impress. White stucco and terra cotta outside, with a tiled lobby, hand-loomed area rugs, and a wrought-iron staircase with herons and ibis on the balusters. In the gift shop, the counter of the soda fountain was a single piece of marble, seventy feet long, chosen by Mr. Ball himself for its fine-grained pattern.

It was the fanciest place Mayola had ever seen.

She had been turned away at the front door, then at a side door, and though she saw none of the usual WHITES ONLY signs, she had figured it out by the time one of the dishwashers let her into the kitchen. He told her to talk to a Mrs. Yancey, pointed through the grease and smoke and clatter of pots a-stirring, through the god-awful heat, to stairs leading to a lower level, where at least it was cooler.

Mrs. Yancey looked tired. She said that the hotel was full

up with movie people, so she *was* hiring, and how old are you, child?

"Sixteen," Mayola said, and stood up straight to show her tallness. She knew she looked even older, but she kept her hands clasped together serious-like, so they wouldn't shake with the lie. Just a bitty lie, 'cause she *would* be sixteen, after school started up again.

Mrs. Yancey nodded and had her sign some papers with her true full name, then gave her a fast tour of all the fancy and told her where to come tomorrow to change into her uniform, eight o'clock in the morning, sharp. "Bennie Mae will show you what to do."

Vergie was standing in the shade of an oak across the parking lot when Mayola came out the kitchen door. "You get it?"

"I did. Cleaning and folding laundry, just like home."

"'Cept you getting paid?"

Mayola smiled. "Three dollars a week, like you said."

"I told you they was—Shooo-eee!" Vergie stopped talking all of a sudden, her eyes big in her head, and pointed to the front walk. A tall man in creased white pants stood under the awning. "It's Tarzan!" Vergie said, excited. "The real life Tarzan."

"Tarzan ain't real," Mayola said. "He's made-up, from a book." She bit her lip. "Edgar Rice Burroughs," she said, and thought in her head that Miz Green would be pleased she remembered that whole name.

"Ain't neither. I seen his picture in a movie magazine at my auntie's house, over to Jacksonville. That's Tarzan hisself, standing right over there."

Mayola watched the man get into a long, shiny car and drive away, fast. Whoever he was, he was about the handsomest white fella she'd ever seen. When the dust had settled back down, she said, "I'm gonna go home. You coming with me?"

"Maybe. Odell don't get off work til six, but it must be close to that. Let's go see if he's done, then he can go a piece of the way with us."

Mayola made a face, but since Odell working here was the only reason she had a job, and Vergie *had* come all this way, it would be rude not to return the favor.

He was down on the dock, leaning casual against a post, wearing his brown uniform shirt with a wide, short tie. His boat-captain hat sat on top of the post. There was a little breeze coming off the water, and the air smelled green with moss and reeds and fish.

"Well, now," Odell said when he saw Vergie. "Hey there." He was most twenty, with a slow, soft way of talking and conked hair that had started to kink up again after the heat of the day. A trickle of oil shone on his neck.

Vergie walked so that her front self stuck out at him, and he was noticing every bit of it. "Hey, O-dell." She tiptoed over, baby steps like her shoes pinched, and he was just about to put his arm around her waist in a way he hadn't ought to when he saw Mayola and put his hands in his pockets instead.

"Eve'nin, Mayola."

"Odell."

No one said a word then, until a frog jumped off the weedy bank with a splash and made enough noise to shoo away the silence.

"You done here?" Vergie asked. "If you is, you can walk me home."

"Not tonight, darlin.'" Odell tossed a flat coil of rope into the boat. "I got to take movie folks out for a sunset cruise, every night this week." He pulled a rag out of his pocket and polished an invisible speck of dust from the shiny brim of his cap.

"When you gonna take *me* out for a boat ride?" Vergie pushed out her lip in a little-girl pout.

"Next week, sometime. I promise. Purty as any picture out there in the moonlight." He smiled, showing all his teeth, and started to give her part of the speech he made for visitors. "WAH-kulla springs. One'a nature's paradise . . . "

Mayola let him go on for a minute, then said, "I got chores at home, Vergie."

"I reckon it's 'bout time." She flounced her skirt a little, so Odell could see her bare knees, then turned and walked off the dock, the soles of her Keds flap-flapping on the damp wood. She hooked her elbow through Mayola's. "Nothing more to do *here.*"

<hr />

Mayola left her house at seven every morning, walking from the Shadeville Road through the cut to Wakulla Springs. The air was warm, but the sun was barely over the trees, so it was mostly shade, and she listened to birds waking up and starting their day. Sometimes she even whistled back. She liked the Lodge all right. The other girls in the kitchen and the laundry were nice and showed her what to do. They sang songs from the radio when no one was around to hear and told stories about the movie people in giggled whispers.

"I was toting lunch down to them crew folk," Annie said, "and one of the men was taping big crepe paper ears onto that elephant. I give Steve—he's the prop boy—I give him the picnic box, and asked him, what for he doing that? You know what he said?"

Mayola shook her head.

"He said that was a Injun elephant, and they got itty bitty ears. But Tarzan, he live in *Af*rica, and elephants there have big ol' floppy ears. So they making it a costume. A costume for a elephant!"

Mayola like to bust up laughing. "Movie folk are plumb nuts."

But the work wasn't too hard. No more than she was used to,

with four brothers and sisters. It was just chores, for more people. Bennie Mae said she picked up the routine quicker any girl she'd had before, which made Mayola feel good inside. By her second week, she was cleaning rooms by herself, unfolding the crisp white sheets that smelled like flower soap, wiping off all the nice smooth sinks and commodes, and dusting the tops of the walnut chiffoniers, careful not to move any of the hairbrushes or wristwatches, not even an inch.

The hotel maids got twenty minutes off for lunch. Most of the girls sat outside the kitchen door to smoke and flirt with boys. But Mayola had discovered a hedge on the other side of the building, where she could sit in the shade and read her book for a bit without anyone bothering her. She looked up, now and then, and watched the movie people playing make-believe.

They had lots of fancy equipment—cameras and lights, and machines she could not imagine the names of. Some were stuck into the ground, and some were on a big raft right out in the river. The boss man sat in a folding chair under a striped umbrella and gave orders to a second boss man, who shouted through a big red cone. "Quiet on the set!"

They had a bunch of animals she'd only seen pictures of before. The elephant, of course, and a cooter turtle the size of a truck tire, and a whole lot of bright-color birds and little brown monkeys. Her favorite was a big monkey they called Cheeta that must have been real smart. It walked upside-down on its hands, and did somersaults, making faces, screeching and hooting like it was trying out people-talk. It liked to jump up onto Mr. Tarzan, and Mr. Tarzan would laugh and take it for a ride. One day she saw Mr. Tarzan give it a cigar to smoke, like it was one of the boys.

Seemed like every day, Mr. Tarzan was up to some kind of prank, hiding one lady's clothes, or putting a piece of wet moss on the second boss man's chair, then laughing his head off. He was a grown man—a *big* grown man—but he acted just like a little kid, sometimes.

Maybe it was because he was a movie star. They had different ideas about manners, Mayola decided. Except for a handful of pretty white ladies in robes and swimming suits, the cast and crew were all men. Some of them were all dressed up like Florida was for-real Africa, in round white helmets and khaki shirts with lots of pockets. But the rest walked around in undershirts, or no shirts at all, and didn't seem the least bit embarrassed to be out in public like that, even in front of the ladies.

On the Wednesday of her second week at the Lodge, Mayola sat under her shrubbery, nibbling on the cornbread and syrup her mama had wrapped up in wax paper for her lunch. She heard a big splash and a lot of shouting, and looked up from her book to see three colored boys swimming just off the dock. *Fools*, she thought. The whole hotel was Jim Crow, and they were going to be in a world of trouble, jumping in that water in broad daylight.

Then she saw Mr. Tarzan swimming with them, ducking them under water, diving down after them. She guessed it must be okay, if *he* wanted them there. Maybe they were playing at being Africans, like the elephant. That made sense, Mayola thought. Africa was where most colored people come from, to begin with.

The boss man yelled "Cut!" and a minute later, Mr. Tarzan and the boys climbed up onto the dock. Two of them flopped down like they was bone-tired, but the third came up onto the lawn and headed for the drinking fountain next to the changing room, not fifteen feet from where Mayola sat.

She skooched back farther under the leaves, making herself invisible, because *that* was asking for real trouble.

And sure enough, he was just bending over the fountain when

one of the gardeners, a Shadeville man named Daniel, looked up from weeding a flowerbed and saw him.

"You, boy! You get away from there!" Daniel jumped up, real fast for a big man, and in two shakes he had grabbed the boy by the scruff of his neck. "What you think you're doing, taking a drink from there?"

The boy looked up, and Mayola sucked in her breath when she saw that he wasn't colored at all. He was one of the lifeguards from Tallahassee who liked to tease the kitchen girls, all done up in greasepaint like a minstrel show.

He pushed Daniel's hands away. "Get your dirty paws off me, *boy*," the lifeguard said, louder than he needed to.

Daniel backed up a step and, after a moment, took his felt hat off. His bald head was dark and shiny with sweat. "Sorry, suh. I didn' mean nothin' by it." Daniel had gone to the A&M for two years, studying to be a teacher until his daddy lost their farm, but he could sure talk field-hand mushmouth when he had to, Mayola thought. The big man continued. "I thought you was, well, suh, I—" He faltered, and wrung his hat in his hands.

The manager of the hotel, Mr. Perry, walked up just then. "Is there a problem?"

The boy's mouth was tight and angry, but before he could say anything, Daniel did.

"My mistake, Mist' Perry. I didn' recognize the young gen'l'man in that make-up."

"Thought he was one of *your* boys, drinking where he shouldn't?"

"Yessuh. 'Zactly that. I'se just about to give him what-for when I seen he was in the right place after all."

"Hmm." Mayola watched Mr. Perry think on that a bit, then turn to the boy. "Get back to the set, Joe. They're ready for the next shot. I'll have someone bring you a Coke."

The boy hesitated, giving Daniel the hairy eyeball, then shrugged and walked off with a swagger, like he had more important things to do.

Daniel worried his hat between his hands, sweat beaded on his forehead.

"There's four young men in costume today," Mr. Perry said. "You'd best be careful." He turned to go back to the dock, but stopped in mid-turn and pointed a finger at the drinking fountain. The faucet was smeared with what looked like shoe polish, one side of the porcelain bowl blotched with an inky handprint.

"And clean that mess up, Danny, before one of the guests sees it."

Daniel replaced his hat and, after a pause, pulled a red rag from the pocket of his bib overalls. "Yes, sir," he told Mr. Perry's retreating back, saying it clearly as two words. A bit more clearly than strictly needed, Mayola noticed.

She waited until the boss was back on the dock before she stood up from behind the bush.

"You been there the whole time, Miss Mayola?"

She nodded. "Eating my lunch." She looked down at the water. They were all swimming again. "I don't get it. They want colored people, why they have to go and paint up white boys? Ain't like we short on colored folk round here. And most looking for work, too."

"I don't know for certain," he said, scrubbing away, "but what I hear is Mr. Ball won't let them."

"How come? It ain't his movie."

"Nope. But it's his water, and, movie or not—" He gave the porcelain fountain one last flick of his rag. "—he doesn't want folks like *us* swimming in it." He touched the brim of his hat to Mayola, and returned to his flowers.

"Shit, Newt. I don't want to go on any boat tour. I spent all day in that goddamn river." Johnny Weissmuller said. He'd worked with Perry on three pictures, and knew he didn't have to put on his company manners.

"I know. But it's the Tallahassee Ladies Club, and they are the lovely wives of the Pork Chop Gang."

"Mr. Ball's friends?"

"Indeed. The stalwart men of commerce and politics who are bringing purity and prosperity to the great state of Florida."

"I get it." Weissmuller sighed. "Smile and look manly." He struck a Tarzan pose.

"That's the ticket." Perry slapped him on the shoulder. "Oh, and by the way, Mr. Ball said I should tell you that he recognizes how valuable your time is, so once the tour is over, you'll find a bottle of Jim Beam waiting in your room."

Weissmuller smiled. "For that, first crocodile we see, I'll even give them the Tarzan yell."

"The nearest croc is almost five hundred miles away, down in the Everglades. They're all alligators, here."

"Same thing." Weissmuller looked down at his slacks. "I don't have to jump in and wrassle one, do I?"

"No, Johnny. *These* animals aren't rubber."

The Jungle Cruise boat was a long, shallow box, open to the air, with five rows of wooden benches. That afternoon it was full of tittering ladies, all hats and gloves and floral cologne. A few of them weren't bad looking. Johnny sat at the back with the boatman, a genial, fixed grin on his face.

The outboard motor started up with a roar and a belch of blue smoke, which dissipated, along with the reek of gasoline, when they were away from the dock. The roar settled into a purr, and

Johnny felt the breeze ruffle the ends of his hair. He'd left it loose, Tarzan-style, for the occasion.

"Good after-noon, ladies," boomed the boatman. "My name is Odell Watkins, and I will be your chauffeur on this fine, fine Florida day."

He had a big voice, and Weissmuller could tell he was starting a speech he'd practiced many times.

"WAH-kulla springs. One'a nature's paradise. Now the crystal clear waters'a this springs flow out of the grawn at more'n a million gallons ever single day, a-formin the Wah-kulla River you now a-floating on. Look there! Over on the right, you see a bird with spread-out wings. That there's the Anhinga, also known as the snake bird, or water turkey. An-hinga!"

The ladies turned, but were watching Tarzan as much as the wildlife, so Weissmuller kept the smile on his face and let his gaze wander. It really was a stunning bit of landscape. He could see why Thorpe wanted to film the location shots here. No sign of modern civilization. The sky was a deep clear blue, and the vegetation was wild, even primitive. It would look African enough on film, even in black-and-white. He wondered if they'd shoot the next picture in color. After *Wizard of Oz* came out, two years ago, it was all anyone talked about. Would they have to remix his makeup? He'd ask one of the—

"Now there's a sight!" Odell said, pulling Johnny back from his reverie. "Four cooter turtles, all a-sitting on the same log like they was waiting for a bus. They got no idea Wah-kulla means waters'a mystery in the language'a the Injuns used to live here. They was here when Mr. Poncey de Leon come up this river four hunnert years ago, a-lookin for the fountain'a youth. He kept a-going, but they's some folks think he done found it right here in these pure waters, and died 'fore he could come back to claim it. Now ever'one, keep you hands *in*-side the boat, cause over there is a big old gator. American alligator, born and raised right here in Florida."

He turned the boat toward the shore, and Johnny saw the dark, ridged back moving slowly through the weeds. That was his cue. He stood up and put one foot on the stern of the boat.

"*Aaahhh-eeeeeeee-aaahhhh-eeeee-aaaahhhh-eeeeee-aaaah-hhhh!*" he yodeled. He saw a few women jump in their seats. Then there were oohs and aahs and giggles and a polite spatter of applause. He gave a small bow, more of a nod, and sat down again. There. That'd give 'em a story for their next meeting.

"If you look to your left," Odell continued, "you'll see the Anhinga, also known as the snake bird, or water turkey. An-hinga!"

The boat cruised down the river about a mile, then turned and came back up on the other side of an enormous stand of towering bald cypress festooned with pale gray moss. Pointing out several more anhingas—snake birds—water turkeys—the increasingly repetitious boatman took them through a back channel, a dark and decidedly swamp-like section, then returned to the open water, directly over the springs.

"Wah-kulla Springs. One'a the biggest and deepest springs in the en-tire world. So clear that when I drop this here penny in—watch now—you can see it shining all the way to the bottom, one hunnert *eight*-y feet below. Under that platform over there is the spot where some diver-mens discovered the drownded skeleton of a wooly mammoth elephant, a pre-storic animal that walked the earth more'n ten *thou*-sand years ago.

"Now, look down to the right. See them stone ledges, all pretty and green and blue? If it was dark, you would see some itty bitty lights a-glowin' down there, too. Ain't no paint or magic, no siree. It just nature's natural beauty." He lowered his voice to a spooky timbre. "There's also an Injun legend says them lights is fairy critters, playing in the deeps. I guess y'all never know what might be a-lurking in them limestone caves."

As if on cue, he was interrupted by a loud wailing sound that raised the hair on the back of Johnny's neck.

"Gracious!" A woman fluttered a handkerchief to her mouth. "What was *that*?"

"That there is the limpkin bird, one'a the rarest birds there is in this state." The boatman lowered his voice again. "There's folks say it sound just like the cry of a woman, lost forever in the swamps."

It was a good line, and Johnny saw that it had its intended effect on the twittering audience. Including him. As they pulled into the dock, he was more than usually comforted by the thought of the bottle waiting in his room.

When Mayola came to work on Thursday morning, a big color poster was propped on an easel in the lobby. *Tarzan and His Mate.* Across one corner, a hand-lettered sign said:

SPECIAL SHOWING!
ON THE PORCH
FRIDAY NIGHT—9:00 PM

The changing room downstairs was all abuzz. A Hollywood movie right in the Lodge! Bennie Mae went to ask Mrs. Yancey if they could see it too, or if it was just for guests. She came back and said since there wasn't a separate balcony, it being a porch, Mrs. Yancey didn't think so. But later that afternoon, when they were polishing the marble tables in the lobby, Mr. Perry walked in, and Bennie Mae walked right over to him, bold as brass, and asked.

He looked a little surprised, but he rubbed his chin, and said that since it was a fine summer evening, he supposed the colored help might enjoy the show too. "I'll have the boatmen bring up some benches, set you up right out on the lawn," he said.

Mayola had never seen a real movie. There wasn't a picture show in Wakulla County, and she had only been to Tallahassee once, for Easter. A traveling preacher had brought *The Life of Jesus* and showed it to the Sunday School, a few years back, but she reckoned that didn't exactly count.

Friday afternoon, a couple of the men from the movie crew set up a big projector machine on the glassed-in porch of the hotel, and hung a white sheet at one end for a screen. Mayola and the other girls stayed in their uniforms after their shift was over and ate sandwiches in the kitchen, then moved all the wicker porch chairs into nice neat rows while the guests had a barbecue supper under the magnolias and the live oaks.

By the time everything was set up, Mayola was tired on her feet and sweaty inside her uniform. The thermometer had inched close to one hundred that day, and the air was just about soup.

She sat down at the end of one of the benches, a few feet from the shrubbery where she ate her lunch, and watched the light change around her. The lawn was still and quiet, no people bustling around. The water looked just like a sheet of glass, with shifting colors beneath it—deep, dark greens and blues dappling the white sand bottom. It made the painted tiles of the lobby seem shabby. The clouds had gone all pink, and they reflected in the water as perfect as any mirror. She felt like she was in some place out of a storybook, not part of the ordinary world, so pretty it like to take her breath away.

The last of the sun touched the very tops of the trees; everything else was shadows. Then even that light faded, the blue of the sky deepened, and stars began to wink on. The moon rose over a bend in the river, and a trickle of white light made a river of its own, sparkling down the middle of the dark water.

All around her the grass and the trees were a-hum with the soft shirring of unseen creatures. Mayola remembered what Odell had said in his tourist voice, about the fairies that lived deep below in the springs. In the daylight, she had known it for a tale, but now it seemed like it might really be true.

The benches began to fill up with the hotel staff. Maids and gardeners and cooks chattered with each other, waiting for the show to begin. Through the arched windows of the lighted porch, Mayola watched the guests come in from the lobby—men in suits and ties, ladies in dresses with flowers and sparkles, all talking and smoking cigarettes. She didn't see Mr. Tarzan, but the little fella they called Boy came in holding the hand of the big monkey that did so many tricks, and they sat right in the front row.

When it was so dark that Mayola couldn't tell where the land ended and the water began, a man turned out the lights on the porch and started up the projector. It whickered so loud it drowned out even the cicadas, and then the sheet was full of a map that said "Darkest Africa." All of a sudden, there was Mr. Tarzan, swinging from tree to tree, yelling his special yell, like he did every morning, out his window, wanting his breakfast.

Too bad Vergie was off dancing with that Odell. She'd be sorry when she heard about all *this*.

Mayola could hear Mr. Tarzan's yell through the glass, but not much of the talking parts, so she just watched the pictures. Mr. Tarzan was in the jungle, with that same funny monkey, and he had visitors—white men in those round hats, with colored boys to carry their bags, just like the hotel. The white men had guns, and got into a big fight with some other colored boys who had spears and not much clothes and mostly got killed. *These* ones weren't white boys in minstrel paint, neither. Mayola leaned forward and looked close, to make sure.

Then Mr. Tarzan was back, with a lady friend. He treated her real nice. Woke her up in the morning by puffing his breath in her hair, gentle-like, and she smiled and they kissed, and she ate striped fruit like little watermelons that grew right on the jungle trees. Then he must have said, "Swim," 'cause the lady smiled again and next thing you know they dived off a tree into water so clear you could watch them underwater.

They swam together like they were playing, like swimming was their most favorite thing in the wide world. She held onto his shoulders, and they dived deep down, and then she took hold of his feet, and they turned slow circles in the water, looking at each other and laughing to make bubbles. Mayola hugged her arms to herself to stop them aching for the want of being able to swim like that.

When the round-hatted men came back, she got up and walked away a piece in the darkness, wanting to keep the swimming part in her head long enough that she'd never forget the picture of it. She walked across the lawn, careful, looking over her shoulder to make sure no one saw. But everyone was too busy watching the make-believe paradise on the screen. Mayola tucked herself deep under the shadow of the diving platform and leaned against a wooden post, a foot from the water.

Out there was the deepest, coolest part, where the spring welled up from underground. She edged a toe close enough to feel the different surface on the sole of her shoe, and half-whispered, "Oh, Lord, I wish I could jump in, just once, and swim like there's no tomorrow."

Johnny Weissmuller smiled and posed for pictures with Mr. Ball's friends, shook hands, and signed autographs all through the picnic supper. But when everyone trooped out to the porch for the screening, he made his excuses: dinner time out in California, want to call my wife before she puts the baby to bed. They were family men and said they understood and patted him on the back as he headed toward the elevator.

Up in his room, he didn't touch the phone. He'd talked to Beryl two days ago and doubted she had anything new to say. It had only been a way to escape having to watch the movie.

Johnny didn't mind seeing himself on screen—since the Olympics there had been so many newsreels and premieres and Hollywood must-shows that he was used to it. It was *this* movie. He'd seen it so many times. And the print they were showing tonight was the one the Hays Office had censored.

They'd made the studio butcher the best scene. Him and Josie, Maureen's stand-in. O'Sullivan couldn't swim a lick. Josie was a beautiful girl who had swum in the '28 games. He'd had his loin-cloth, of course, but she'd worn nothing at all when they shot it at Silver Springs. Tarzan and Jane, skinny-dipping at dawn. Innocent fun. Art, even.

A week later, the word had come down to reshoot, with "Jane" fully-suited, for theaters in less-sophisticated markets. That was bad enough, but seven years later, it seemed the whole country had gone puritan. The League of Decency had made sure that scene was chopped and chopped until it was almost unrecognizable. He couldn't stand to look at it.

Weissmuller paced the length of the little provincial hotel room. Fidgety energy. He looked at the bottle of bourbon on the night-stand, but shook his head. What he needed was to get in the water, really kick it loose. He stripped, put on his trunks, and slipped into khakis and a loose shirt, grabbed his wallet and keys. He went down the side stairs, skirting the lobby for the parking lot door and walked around the building, making a wide swing to avoid the flickering porch. He whistled under his breath when he was clear, like he was playing hooky.

Even with the moonlight, he might not have noticed the tall colored girl, deep in the shadows of the diving platform, if he hadn't heard her whispered prayer. He smiled. Didn't matter if she was just one of the maids. Tonight, she was someone else who wanted to swim.

Bare feet padding over the soft grass, quiet as a jungle hunter, he stepped over to a canvas tent a dozen yards away. He helped himself to Newt's sister's costume, hanging on the line to dry, and returned to the platform.

Johnny Weissmuller held out his hand. "So, you want to swim?"

<hr/>

Mayola nearly jumped out of her skin when she heard the man's voice a few feet away. She was caught, and nowhere to run. Taking a deep breath, she stood straight up and stepped out to take her medicine. "Sorry, suh. I was lookin' at the water, tha's all. I didn—"

Then she stopped, because it wasn't Mr. Perry or one of his men. It was Mr. Tarzan. Mr.—Mr. Weissmuller.

"Come. Swim with me," he said. He held out a piece of cloth.

She stared at him for long enough to feel the rudeness of it before she spoke. "S'cuse me?"

"Swim with me. I brought you a suit." He took a step forward and draped it over her arm.

Mayola recognized it as the jungle suit one of the pretty women wore. She smoothed her hand over it, soft as a baby's blanket on her arm, and thought how it would feel on the rest of her skin, to wear something that fine. Then she came to her senses, and handed it back. "I can't."

"I'll teach you. I taught Boy to swim. Little John."

"No sir, it ain't that." Mayola shook her head. "I been swimming since I was knee high. Just like a fish, my daddy says. I can—" She stopped before pride got her tongue wagging too much.

"Good. Then come swim."

"Not in Mr. Ball's springs, sir." Mayola watched his face twitch in puzzlement, then remembered he wasn't from around here. "Colored people ain't allowed."

He stared at her for a long minute, with an odd expression, like that was a brand-new idea coming into his brain. Then he looked away, out over the water, and when he looked back, he held the suit out again, his face all a-grin.

"Tarzan not care for white man's law."

Mayola sighed. If only it was that easy. Because she wanted to, as much as anything she'd ever pined over in the Sears Christmas wishbook. Wanted to dive into that clear water and swim just like the lady in the movie.

But this wasn't pretend.

"Thank you, sir, but no," she said out loud with her mouth while the rest of her was busy imagining how it would be. "If anyone was to see, I'd lose my job." She stroked the suit again, then sighed deep into her true self, and said, softer, "It's a good job, and I'm saving the money. I'm gonna go up to the Florida A&M some day."

She waited for him to laugh like everyone else, chuckle at her biggity dreams. But he didn't. He just looked at her with those big, dark eyes.

"I never went to college," he said after a moment. "I had to work, and then I was swimming." He sounded sad about it, and put his hands in his pockets. He took a step away, then a step right back, and next thing she knew, he was nodding, like someone had asked him a question.

"Here," he said, pulling out a leather wallet. He counted out some bills, tucking them into the pocket of her uniform, and grinned again, like a little boy about to do mischief. "Insurance. In case we get caught."

"Oh, no, sir! I can't—"

"Call it a scholarship." He put his hand on the small of her back and gave her a gentle little push toward the tent. "Umgawa! Girl change now. Swim with Tarzan."

Mayola walked over to the movie tent, as slow as if her feet were thinking. She liked to set with an idea a bit before she started off to do it, but there wasn't much time for that. She glanced up at the porch. No one was looking. No one was paying any attention to her at all, except Mr. Tarzan.

How many times a movie star gonna ask you to dance? she asked herself. That was what it felt like. Not some jook joint, as loud and hot and sweaty as working. Another kind of dancing, one she knew didn't come round every day.

Mayola *wanted* this dance.

It was against the rules. Mr. Ball's rules. She felt a little bundle of angry grow hot inside her. Mr. Ball didn't make that beautiful water. He just bought the land. Under the law, that was all it took. But it didn't feel right, under the moonlight.

Ain't nobody own the moon.

She unbuttoned her gray uniform, stiff with sweat, and started to fold it up neat, then let it slide down to the ground. Mr. Ball's uniform, too. She heard the pocket crinkle, and took out the money. A hundred dollars! More than eight *months'* pay. She stood with it in her hand, letting the night air blow warm on all of her skin, then rolled the bills tight and tucked them into the toe of her shoe next to her lucky penny. Just in case.

Mayola pulled on the baby-soft swim suit and felt like a movie star herself. She looked down at her long legs and smiled, then stepped barefoot out into the summer night, to dance in the water with Tarzan.

He was waiting by the platform in a pair of trunks. He whistled. "Girl pretty. Swim now." He dived in with barely a splash.

Mayola hesitated with one more moment of last-second thoughts, then took a deep breath and followed.

After the heat of the day and the sweat and the closeness of the swamp air, the water was everywhere cool silk on Mayola's skin. She swam hard, feeling the bubbles tickle back along her body, and when she came up for air a minute later, she was out in the middle of the deepest water.

She could make out the twisted shapes of the cypress on the far bank, hung ghostly with Spanish moss, could separate out trees and ground and gently moving water. On the other side, across the dark grass, the flicker of the projector made the porch look like a glass cage.

Mayola felt the water swirl around her before she saw him surface and ask in a quiet voice, "Can you open your eyes, under?"

She nodded, before she remembered it was dark. "Yes, sir."

"Good." Tarzan took her hand. "Dive now."

They went deep into the springs. The surface above her became a flat ceiling, backlit by the moon. The water was like crystal. She could see all around her, watch her hands move in front of her face, see the paler sleekness of the man swimming beside her.

He tugged and pointed and she looked down. Her mouth opened in a surprised O that let out a stream of fat bubbles, but she didn't let herself gasp water. Below her, the rocks of Wakulla

Springs glittered with tiny lights. Almost green, almost—no color she could put a name to—they sparkled like underwater stars as she moved.

The two swimmers came up to the surface like turtles, nibbling at the air, then sinking back down. He took hold of her feet, his hands big enough to close all around, and they turned circles under the water, just like in the movie. With every turn, every cascade of bubbles, Mayola felt a little bit of bed-making and laundry and sticky hot Florida leave her body and float up and away.

Out here, the water that had looked so still from the shore was always moving, a slow current that eddied around her, over her, bobbing her from side to side. When she surfaced, treading water for a minute, she cupped her hands around the reflection of a tiny round moon; it skittered across her palm like a droplet on a hot stove.

She didn't know how long they'd been swimming, had lost count of how many times they'd come up for air and dived down again. They had swum and floated downstream from the deep springs to a stretch of pure white sand only six feet below the surface. Tarzan swam into a hollow log, came out the other side and touched her arm. *Tag, you're it.*

In and out, out and in, up for air. Mayola felt like she was in a dream. She rose into the stripe of moonlight in the center of the river, and a moment later, he popped up beside her, his long dark hair fanning out with the current.

"Race?" he said. He pointed to a fallen tree that angled into the water beyond the bulk of the boat dock. She nodded, and set off with a long stroke and a strong kick.

She had raced the boys before, at the Sink and in the river—and won—but she had never in her whole life swum as hard as this.

Nothing existed but the joy of her body in the water, legs and arms pulling all of a piece.

She knew he must have held back some; he was the best swimmer in the world. But he didn't let her win, either. They pulled up on the bank at the same time, panting and grinning to beat the band. He climbed up onto a little sandy ledge above the weeds and reached out for her waist, pulling her up next to him.

Mayola lay on the sand, breathing ragged for a minute, feeling that good tired that comes from pushing against all the edges. The air moving across her wet skin was cool and warm at the same time, and she stretched into the comfort of it, one hand floating on the surface of the water, heels furrowing the sand.

"Girl swim good," Tarzan said. He lay inches away, propped up on one muscular arm. Rivulets of water dripped from his hair; in the moonlight, they made glistening silver trails across his smooth skin.

She looked over at his face. He was smiling, his eyes crinkled at the corners. She smiled back, a feeling of dreamy peacefulness stealing over her. They were the only people in the world, and they had shared something beyond the telling of it.

He lowered his head to the sand, facing her. "Girl happy?"

"Yes."

"Good." He stroked her hair, pulling him toward her. "Tarzan happy, too."

Mayola Williams lay her head on Tarzan's chest, his arms strong around her. He pressed his lips lightly to her forehead, and she didn't move, but closed her eyes and sighed deep into herself, listening to his heartbeat and the calm lapping of the water, the tranquil stillness broken only once by the wailing cry of a limpkin.

2

THE
BEASTIE

U NDERWATER WAS THE BEST. ON THE SURFACE, SURE, he gained some speed, but the sun was too hot, and with all the splashing he couldn't see much above or below. If he slowed down or treaded water he was too easily spotted, at risk of a thrashing at best and, at worst, a call to the sheriff. When he was both deep and still, he might as well have been a rock, or a bass, or a mastodon's jawbone, for all the notice he attracted from the kids above, the ones confined to the swimming area, the ones who didn't live here.

Levi liked to creep surefooted along the rock face—his toes seeming almost to stick froglike to the ridges, fixing himself there, crouched and bobbing—and watch the swimmers overhead, the girls especially. Against the sun-bright surface their shapes should have been featureless black cutouts, but the light seemed to shine through them, illuminate them from inside, the way the color photos of mossy trees and egrets shone brightly in their backlit brass frames on the Lodge's lobby walls, getting brighter as the sun set and the wood and marble darkened all around them.

In the H. G. Wells story the boy had read five times, light passed through a scientist and made him the Invisible Man. The boy didn't know what kind of sun H. G. Wells had in England, but when Florida sun passed through the girls on the surface of Wakulla

Springs they became more visible than ever before. Certainly more visible than they had been last year. The boy was what his mama called "going on twelve"—which wasn't as good as straight-up twelve but sure beat the hell out of eleven—and the light at going-on-twelve must be different somehow, because whenever two or more girls were overhead, he could not look away from their floating, somersaulting, shoulder-straddling, bubbling, daz-zling blue-green brightness.

As a result, almost without noticing, he was getting better and better at holding his breath. Not until the last possible moment did he allow himself to kick off from the ledge, across and down into the friendly cool rush from the cave mouth that propelled him forward, far beneath the floating rope that fenced the tourists. He had learned to stop kicking when the springs swept him up, to allow himself to be flung across the water, until he was only a few lazy strokes from surfacing amid the weeds on the far bank. There he hopped onto his favorite cypress stump—though its knees no longer fit his butt so well and its bulk no longer hid him so easily from the waterfront—and shook his head like Big Man Jackson's coon hound, spraying underground water in all directions.

"That boy's half fish," Big Man had said in the boathouse one day, while the boy lay on the dock, eavesdropping beneath the window. Levi had flushed so hot and heavy with pride that he might have burned through the boards and dropped into the river hissing and steaming, like a stray coal from the stove. Now he perched on the knobby stump and screwed fingers into his ears to scrub out the water and heard the far-side swim-sounds—"Marco! Polo!"—and wondered, not for the first time, what a *colored* girl would look like suspended in the water between the Florida sun and the bottom of the springs.

He knew, of course, what his friends looked like in the Sink.

That's where he'd first learned to swim, paddling around at an age when other younguns were just learning to walk, or so he'd been told. But Wakulla had a light entirely different from the Sink's, and he could talk none of the Shadetown girls into dipping so much as a toe into *these* springs, not under cover of the new moon.

"You gonna get your fool self killed," they told him.

But he wasn't killed yet. In fact, he was hungry. Maybe Aunt Vergie would give him a piece of cornbread, if he looked dry and presentable and less like what the cook called "a naked Injun."

Levi crept through the woods on the western shore of the springs until he reached his dry clothes, tucked amid the branches of a fallen pignut hickory. This was no wad of clothing but a carefully folded square. Levi's mama ironed his next day's clothes every night, and she gave him strict orders not to walk around looking "chewed." His daily disobedience of his mama's sternest warning— "You stay out of that white swimming hole, you hear? I lose this job, we got no place to live, and you and me will be thumbing to Orlando."—made him all the more determined to mind her other rules. She always said "Orlando" as if the town were the back of beyond, so Levi had a notion that his cousins there must be living in upended packing-crate sheds beneath the orange trees, and fighting the crows for food.

He carefully unfolded the bundle and gently shook out his shirt and pants, looking for chiggers, before putting them on. Then he laced his shoes, propping each foot in turn against the hickory trunk. He brushed some bits of bark off his shirt and headed through the woods again, angling away from the water so he wouldn't come out at the diving platform, as crowded as the Tallahassee train station, even during the off-season. Instead he ducked beneath a stand of towering magnolias, their gnarled bottom limbs and great greasy leaves hanging nearly to the ground, and walked in a crouch along his cool secret path, shared by raccoons and other night creatures. He liked to imagine that swamp panthers crouched in the limbs overhead and watched him pass, not attacking because they knew Levi was their friend and would never bother them, or maybe because the heat of the day just made them drowsy.

He emerged onto the entrance road and sighed with relief, both because the warmth of the setting October sun was welcome on his face and arms and because he no longer needed to be quite so furtive as he headed back toward the Lodge. Levi wasn't nearly as dark as many of the Shadetown children—"high-yaller" was what they called his coppery skin, though not when Levi's mother was around—but he was plenty colored enough that his breaching the surface in the middle of the swimming area would empty the beach as quickly as a sea monster.

Out here, though, rich visitors off the highway were actually pleased to see a neatly dressed colored boy strolling along the shoulder of Mr. Ball's newly paved mile-long drive. He was a part of the exotic Florida landscape they had traveled to see, like an ibis in the marsh or a gator in the ditch. They figured he was on his way to bus tables or shine shoes at the Lodge. Sometimes they stopped to take his picture and, less frequently, give him a nickel.

But the road was deserted at the moment, it being a Sunday afternoon, so Levi was in his preferred state: alone with his imaginings. As he walked, he repeatedly pulled an imaginary gun on an invisible saboteur, pretending he was Herbert A. Philbrick, hero of *I Led Three Lives*—Levi's favorite TV show—on assignment to infiltrate a Communist cell headquartered at the Wakulla Springs Lodge. It could happen. Famous people had stayed there—though his mama didn't like to talk about them much—and weren't those the most likely targets of Soviet assassins? Famous people? Ordinary people just got killed.

Given this morbid line of thought, he was spooked when a voice called out behind him:

"Big House, Mister! I got your Big House!"

It was just Policy Sam, hurrying to catch up. As usual, he paid little attention to where he was going, focused instead on recounting the dozens of strips of paper he clutched, plucking them out of one fist and sorting them between the fingers of the other. As he ran, stumbling once or twice, the strips fluttered in the breeze like tails of Spanish moss. "Oh, it's you," Policy Sam said when he caught up. His disappointment was obvious: He knew Levi's mama would whale both of them if she ever caught her boy wasting good money playing the numbers.

Policy Sam had been simply Sam when the boys were growing up, but Levi hadn't seen him at the Sink for more than a year, since Sam had been hired as a runner for old Cooper, up at the Crawfordville Big House. Every boy in the area knew that once he was old enough to do the math, he could earn pocket money running numbers. Young boys were easy to overlook and hard to apprehend; they also were easy to hurt if they got caught pocketing more than the five percent due them. After a few weeks, once they realized the boss expected them to hawk numbers to everyone they met morning, noon, and night, most boys tired of the racket. But Sam always had been a motormouth, and the twenty-four-hour sales pitch suited him. Now everyone called him Policy Sam, and Levi could seldom get him to talk about anything else.

"Good day today?" Levi asked.

"Middling," Sam replied. "But no interesting numbers. Everybody's playing 19 and 53, for the year, or 18 because it's 1-9-5-3 added together, or 5 because the Yankees have won five straight series, or 16 because that's how many series they've won total, or 13 because the Yankees won game six 4 to 3, or—"

"Okay, okay, I get it," Levi said. "Hard to surprise you with a number these days."

"Folks ain't even trying," Sam said. "The dull ones, they play the same number every day. Your Aunt Vergie, I know you love her, but it's always 3 with her, 'cause her little girl was three when she died. Ain't that the sorriest-ass reason for picking a number you ever heard? Some Policy, betting on the age of a little dead girl?"

"Three's a lucky number, too," Levi said.

"Not for her," Sam replied. "You been in swimming?"

"Yeah. How you know that?"

"You digging in your ears like there's water in there," Sam said. He laughed. "And I know your mama didn't give you no bath, 'cause it ain't Saturday."

Levi shoved him, but laughed, too. "Get out! My mama don't wash me. I do that myself."

"Yeah, washing in Mr. Ball's water. I bet you pee in it, too."

"I do not!" Levi said, although he had, some times.

"You know the white people do," Sam said. "When you're paddling around in there, and the water gets warm all of a sudden, that's what it is. You just swam through some white girl's pee."

"Shut up!" Levi said, shoving him again. This time Sam shoved him back, his paper strips fluttering, and the boys continued to laugh and pummel each other, all the way down the drive to the edge of the parking lot, then through the pyracantha hedge to the cigarillo-smoky picnic table where the dishwashers hung out. In an instant, Sam straightened up and resumed his chant, ready to do business. Levi shook his head and went on into the kitchen, which was loud and crowded and so dinner-hour crazy that he could sneak up on Aunt Vergie, reach around her considerable bulk, and snatch away a biscuit before she was able to bust him one.

"Boy, I declare!" Vergie yelled. "You're going to draw back a nub one day."

"Can I help?" he asked, perching on a stool and biting off half the biscuit.

"You better, if you're going to wait here till your mama's done. She's got extra rooms to do tonight. Go bring me a fresh butter brush out of the rack back yonder. This one's losing whiskers."

Levi wedged the biscuit's second half into his mouth as he hopped down on his errand. The first half of a biscuit was to gulp; the second half was to savor. He dodged a half-dozen kitchen employees on the way across the room, saying hey to each, snatched up a brush, and dodged all the same people on the way back, as they said hey to him in return.

"Here you go," he said, resuming his perch. "How come the extra rooms?" But all Vergie heard was a mouthful of biscuit dough, so he swallowed and repeated himself.

"Movie people," she said, spreading melted butter onto a fresh tray of biscuits. "Some of them here already, and they're eating biscuits like they never saw one before. Maybe they ain't. No telling what they eat in California."

Levi's eyes went wide. "What movie people? Are they famous? Are they making another Tarzan movie?"

Aunt Vergie drew back and hissed like a snake. "God almighty, boy, don't say that name when your mama's nigh."

Levi sighed. What his mama liked and didn't like was a mystery sometimes. "I'm sorry, Auntie. What movie are they making?"

"Do I know these things? Do I look like Mr. Edward Ball?" She shook her head and went back to her work. "Go run this tray over to the window, quick now."

This Levi did with great enthusiasm, since Aunt Vergie wasn't the only source of information in the Lodge kitchen. While helping Jamie sweeten the tea, he learned it wouldn't be a full movie crew, just the underwater unit. While helping Bess stir the gravy, he learned filming was to start in a couple of days, if the damned camera would just cooperate. While helping Libby slice the lemons, he learned the camera was complicated because this would be a 3-D movie—just like *House of Wax*, with stuff reaching out in the audience's faces—only this would be an *underwater* 3-D movie. And while helping Howard chop the lettuce, he learned the star of the movie—titled *Black Lagoon*—was Richard Widmark.

"It ain't Richard Widmark, neither," said old Mr. Adderly the roast chef, the wrinkles in his forehead even deeper than usual as he sawed a beef. "Don't lie to the boy." Having passed the thickest, reddest section, halfway through the joint, Mr. Adderly took a break. He set down his two-pronged fork and his angry-looking knife and mopped his streaming face with a handkerchief. He took no notice of the new girl who whisked away the fresh slices; serving was beneath Mr. Adderly. His hands had got to shaking bad, Levi noticed, without a knife to steady them.

"It is so Richard Widmark," Howard said, cracking a celery stalk for emphasis. "My cousin Arthur was polishing the lobby floor when Mr. Ball come out of the office after taking the call, and he said so."

Mr. Adderly pointed at Howard with the fork while Levi stood wide-eyed, looking back and forth. Howard the pantry chef was in charge of the salads, and was the biggest man in the kitchen, his shoulders so broad he had to go through the dining-room door sideways. He also hunted year-round, and could clean and dress any wild animal; Levi was partial to his deer jerky. Levi knew Howard aspired to be roast chef, and Mr. Adderly knew it, too. "You ain't the only one Arthur talks to," Mr. Adderly said. "I got Arthur his job, when you was half the size of Levi here. And Arthur told me it was some other Richard. I just can't remember his name right off."

"Please don't point with sharp things, Mr. Adderly, honey," called Aunt Vergie, dropping coins into Policy Sam's outstretched palm.

Mr. Adderly resumed his carving. "It wasn't Richard Widmark, I know that. It wasn't Richard Burton." He looked up. "I tell you who it is. Richard—What's-His-Name." When Howard looked unimpressed, he went on: "You know. The one who's on that TV show, about the Communist spy."

Levi gasped and dropped a deviled egg with a wet smack. "You mean Richard Carlson?"

"Yeah, that's the one."

Herbert A. Philbrick himself, right here at Wakulla Springs! Why, this very minute he could be in—

Levi slid the deviled eggs into the fridge, ran to the dining-room door, and waited for the right-hand door to clear. First rule: the left-hand door is for getting *in* to the kitchen, the right-hand door for getting out, and Levi didn't want his face mashed in by mistake. A second later, he poked his head out for a quick survey of the forbidden world beyond.

Checkerboard tile gleamed beneath the chandeliers. Dressed-up white people filled every round table, all crystal and silk and shiny shoes, their light talk and laughter floating into the ceiling. A half-dozen colored people dressed in white uniforms moved among the tables with trays, bottles, and sweating pitchers. Levi registered the staff members automatically—Charlie, Winnie, Bud, Wash, Edith, a cute girl he didn't know; W.A. must be sick again, because Bud was working the window tables, too—but focused on the diners, and recognized none of them. Maybe Richard Carlson hadn't arrived yet.

Someone grabbed his collar and yanked him backward from

the doorway into the familiar steamy hubbub of the kitchen, just as one of the busboys swept past, empty bin on hip, opening the swinging door with his butt.

"Why you always in people's way?" asked Levi's mama. She sounded tired and cranky, as she did so often, but her eyes danced to see him, and as she complained, her hands deftly straightened his collar, smoothed his hair, and dusted his shirt, none of which needed doing. "You know I don't come in from the dining room. Why didn't you wait out on the picnic table? C'mere." She hugged him tight. She smelled like detergent and Clorox and clean laundry, with a layer of sweat beneath.

He knew better than to mention the movie people. "It's too smoky out there," he said, "and besides, Sam wouldn't leave me alone." Sam was nowhere to be seen by then, being even more afraid of Levi's mama than of the sheriff, but Levi knew this would score him some points.

"You tell that Sam, he bothers my boy, he'll have to deal with me. Here, Vergie fixed our plates. Carry them for me, will you? You don't have to open them, just carry them. Nosy thing. Yes, it's roast beef, and it's off the end, like you'd eat it any other way. Tell Mr. Adderly thank-you on the way out. Vergie, honey, I'll see you tomorrow."

"'Night, Mayola."

Levi said good night to everyone as he swept in his mama's wake back through the kitchen and out into the yard. The warm covered dishes in his arms smelled good and felt good, too; he was suddenly hungry. The sun had gone down, and only lightning bugs lit the way to the staff dormitory, but his mother was easy to follow, as she talked about her day. He tromped through the gravel behind her.

As they skirted the dense wood of the little sinkhole south of the

Lodge, Levi imagined that from the midst of the thicket, Old Joe, Wakulla's largest gator, watched them pass. Levi hoped Old Joe would recognize Levi for what he was—a fellow water creature, deserving of respect—and therefore would not eat him, should their paths ever cross.

"Levi, are you listening to me?"

"Yes'm," he quickly lied.

"Then why don't you answer? I said, aren't you excited that he'll be here tomorrow? He's been asking after you, says he looks forward to seeing you."

Levi had no idea who his mother meant, though he was pretty sure it wasn't Richard Carlson.

"Yeah," Levi said, tentatively. It seemed a safe thing to say.

"You oughta be," she said. "Jimmy Lee Demps don't come home from Korea every day."

Levi sighed. He might have guessed, since she had scarcely talked about anyone else since her boyfriend's last airmail arrived. Levi could feel his appetite drying up, the covered dishes becoming a burden. He was not inclined to share his mama, certainly not with that fast-talking so-and-so. He looked wistfully back at the spot where he had imagined Old Joe lurking, and silently urged the gator to emerge tomorrow and take care of Jimmy Lee Demps in one gulp. But Old Joe didn't answer, assuming he was there at all, and Levi had no choice but follow his mama back to their apartment, eat a little dinner, wash up, and go to bed, falling asleep into a series of happy dreams about monsters.

The next afternoon, Levi's mama made him dress in his church clothes to meet Jimmy Lee, and insisted further that they walk down the drive to meet his taxi.

"He called the kitchen from the Trailways station in Tallahassee an hour ago," she said as they walked along, looking at her new Timex for the umpteenth time. Mr. Ball liked to give gifts to valued employees, especially wristwatches; they encouraged punctuality. "So he ought to be here any minute, if he found a colored taxi fast. Poor man, riding all the way from Fort Rucker on the bus. He must be wore out."

"How will we know his cab from anyone else's?" asked a grumpy Levi, kicking gravel into the weeds as he trudged along. He was determined to scuff his shoes as much as possible.

"He'll know *me*, silly," his mama said, though she sounded suddenly unsure, and Levi felt a pang of conscience for worrying her. She looked girlish in a bright green dress that swayed just below her knees. She had wanted to wear the heels that matched, but switched to a pair of canvas flats when she realized they'd have to walk almost a mile down and back, and might have a long wait at the highway.

"Gone two years next month," she said. "It seems even longer than that. Thank God Ike ended the war, else Jimmy Lee might be there yet." She rubbed Levi's head. "You were just a little boy when he left."

"He never paid me no mind anyway," Levi said. "He just pretended I wasn't around when he—"

"Oh, Lord, here he comes," his mama said, cutting him off. She waved both arms overhead, and the oncoming cab swerved to the shoulder. Jimmy Lee was out of the car before it came to a stop. He was in full-dress uniform, though Levi's mama knocked his hat off hugging him. Levi picked it up and held it, not sure what to do, while the adults kissed. He glimpsed some medals before he looked away. The taxi driver, a colored man with white stubbly hair, smiled at Levi.

"That hat fit you?" The driver gestured for Levi to try it on. Levi reluctantly perched it atop his head, surprised that it only dropped partway across his eyes.

"Yeah, you at that big-head stage," the driver said. "Don't worry, the rest'll catch up soon enough. A-ha, ha, ha."

Levi glared at him.

"Hey, Levi, thanks," Jimmy Lee said, snatching the hat off the boy's head with his free hand and brushing it on his uniform pants. His other hand was around the waist of Levi's mama. "Can't have my parade duds getting dirty, can I? Pretty gals won't flag me down in the road anymore." Levi's mama kissed him again.

"Y'all might as well hop in," the driver said. "Only what, half a mile, I reckon. No extra charge."

Levi's mama hopped into the backseat with Jimmy Lee—hopped *onto* Jimmy Lee, it seemed to Levi. He slid into the front seat beside the driver, whose big belly was dented by the steering wheel like a cushion. In front of Levi, taped to the dash, were a half-dozen faded magazine photos of Lena Horne, aging from left to right. The man thunked the car into gear and pulled forward, asking the rear-view mirror, "Employee dorm, right?"

"No, sir," Jimmy Lee said. "You pull right up to the main entrance."

"Main entrance?" asked Levi's mama.

"Can't let just you and Levi see me looking this fine, can I?" Jimmy Lee asked. "Got to show off a bit."

The driver squinted at the mirror. "They expecting you, son?"

"They ought to be," Jimmy Lee said. "I got a reservation."

"Oh, my God," Levi's mama said. "You ain't still on about that, are you? Jimmy Lee, this is Florida, not Korea."

"I know where I am," he retorted. "And I know where I've been, and what I've seen—"

"You like baseball?" the driver asked Levi, loudly, as his mama and Jimmy Lee started talking all at once, voices raised. "Boy, I hated to see the Dodgers lose, didn't you? But Campanella, he sure had him a season. One hundred forty-two RBIs, can you imagine? New team record. You play baseball?"

"I swim," Levi said.

"Wish I could swim," the driver said. "Throw me in that swamp over there, I'd sink like a rock. I might as well—"

"Roy Campanella!" Jimmy Lee cried out, interrupting the driver. "Now there's an example for the boy. Larry Doby. Jackie Robinson. Six colored players in the major leagues now." He looked at Levi's mama. "See, times change, baby. And people like us, we're going to keep changing them."

"Jimmy Lee, you could get me fired! And where would we be then?"

"Orlando," Levi murmured.

At the fork, the driver slowed nearly to a stop before he turned left toward the Lodge, shaking his head. He followed the woodcut arrow labeled CHECK IN; the right-hand drive toward the dorm and other outbuildings was unmarked. The backseat quarrel raged as the familiar red tile roof swung into view. "Soldier, you making a big mistake," the driver said.

"Mind your own business, old man," Jimmy Lee replied.

With an *erk*, the driver slammed on brakes, a few yards shy of the turnaround at the front door. Levi braced himself against Lena Horne. There was silence from the back seat as the driver flexed his fingers on the steering wheel, threw the gearshift into Park, then slowly turned toward Levi, the cracked seat leather creaking as he shifted.

"Listen," Jimmy Lee said. "I'm sorry."

The driver ignored him and addressed himself to Levi, who

was trying to smooth down one ragged Lena Horne corner, where his palms had crimped it. "Son, could you help me with this luggage?"

"Yessir," Levi said.

Everyone got out. The driver opened the trunk, and he and Levi hauled out a bulging duffel bag and a battered suitcase that used to have stickers on it, but now just had fuzzy tacky outlines. Jimmy Lee awkwardly held a wad of bills out to the driver, who waited a beat before he accepted it.

"Keep the change," Jimmy Lee said, as the driver reached for his wallet.

"You watch your ass," the driver told Jimmy Lee. He turned to Levi's mama and said, "You have a good evening, ma'am. And you, son," he added as he turned to Levi, "you take care of your mama, you hear?"

"Yessir."

"And keep on swimmin'. But work in a little baseball, too, okay? Ain't never heard of no colored swimmers." By now he was back behind the wheel. He made a three-point turn, waved at Levi, shouted, "You look like an outfielder to me," and was gone.

Levi's mother had her arms folded across her chest. Jimmy Lee reached for her hand, but she shrugged it off.

"Baby," he said, "I need you with me."

"I been praying for you every night for two years, Jimmy Lee Demps," Levi's mama said. "And I will not stand here and watch you get yourself killed now, right on the doorstep of home." She turned and strode toward the dormitory road. "Come on, Levi," she called over her shoulder.

"Dammit," Jimmy Lee muttered. He picked up his luggage in each hand and strode off, toward the front door.

Levi wanted to see what was going to happen. He thought quickly and called to his mama, "Aunt Vergie asked me to come by the kitchen."

His mama slowed her steps, but didn't stop. "All right," she said. "But you stick to the kitchen, and you come *right* back, you hear?"

"Yes'm," Levi said. He waited until she was out of sight before running to the outside fire escape and galloping up, steel steps drumming beneath the leather soles of his Sunday shoes. He'd be less noticeable, he hoped, if he watched from the back-stair landing that overlooked the front desk. The upstairs hall was clear; guests not at the early dinner seating would still be in the water, enjoying the last of the sun. Levi ran to the back stairs, crept down to the landing and crouched there, peering around an iron heron on the balustrade just as Jimmy Lee strode up to the front desk, set down his suitcase and his duffel bag, and placed his fingertips on the mahogany as if it were a set of piano keys. He focused on the desk clerk, looking neither left nor right.

Mr. Teale was on duty this evening, the back of his gleaming bald head turned to the lobby, and to Jimmy Lee. He was shoving messages into numbered cubbyholes, the swinging silver chain on his glasses reflecting the harsh fluorescent bulb of the desk lamp.

The lobby held a handful of people: two white men and a woman in a distant cluster of lounge chairs, holding drinks, all dressed for tennis; Miss Carla in her gray uniform, white hat and apron, polishing the brass photo frames; Mr. Hubert in his red jacket, waxing the floor of the enclosed porch.

All stared at Jimmy Lee, who paid them no mind.

He cleared his throat.

"Oh, I *am* sorry, sir," Mr. Teale said, turning as he spoke. "How may I help—you?" His voice faltered as he looked Jimmy Lee up and down, as if the colored man were a marvel the balding white clerk had never seen before.

"I have a reservation," Jimmy Lee said.

Mr. Teale didn't immediately say anything, though his mouth was slightly open, exposing his crowded lower teeth. He ducked his head and looked over the top of his bifocals at Jimmy Lee.

"I beg your pardon?" he finally said.

Though quiet, the men's voices carried far across the checkerboard tile of the lobby. The five other adults present didn't even pretend not to listen, though Miss Carla continued to make circular polishing motions on the same brass corner, and Mr. Hubert continued to push the waxer back and forth, as if it were a baby long since rocked to sleep.

"I have a reservation," Jimmy Lee repeated. "Made it by phone just last week. The name is Jim—no." He straightened his shoulders. "The name is James Lee Demps. D-E-M-P-S." When Mr. Teale didn't respond, Jimmy Lee added, "I believe it's right there on your card file." He smiled. "I learned to read upside down in the Army. It's useful, when the C.O. calls you in."

"I'm sure it is," Mr. Teale said, plucking the card out of the file and holding it gingerly between his thumb and forefinger, looking back and forth from it to Jimmy Lee. "I'm very sorry, Mr. Demps. I was not on duty to take your call, but there must have been some mistake."

"What do you mean?" asked Jimmy Lee.

"Isn't it obvious, Mr. Demps?" Mr. Teale shook his head. "I mean, you can't stay here."

Jimmy Lee frowned, but only a little. Levi wondered if he had taken up poker in the Army, too. "You have no vacancies?"

"Vacancies are irrelevant, Mr. Demps. The Lodge is—restricted. I'm sorry if you were told otherwise."

"Oh!" Jimmy Lee said. "You mean it's just for white people."

Mr. Teale winced. "If you must put it that way, yes. Whoever you spoke to on the phone must have thought—well, as I say, a mistake was made. I am truly sorry."

Jimmy Lee glanced around the lobby. He pointed first at Miss Carla, then at Mr. Hubert, both of whom quickly turned away. "*She's* not white," Jimmy Lee said, "and *he's* not, either." His pointing finger half lifted, he turned to the gaping tennis players, as if their white-on-whiteness were momentarily in doubt, but only smiled at them before turning back to Mr. Teale.

"The sass of that nigger," one of the men said.

"Where's the Klan when you need 'em?" said the other.

"Those are *employees*, Mr. Demps," Mr. Teale said, raising his voice as if to drown out the murmured ugliness across the room. "As you well know." He cleared his throat. "Now, there are some very nice colored boarding houses between here and Tallahassee. I'm sure our kitchen staff would be pleased to tell you all about them, and we will even call a taxicab on your behalf, if you'll just step around to the delivery entrance."

"Do you see these?" Jimmy Lee pointed to the row of decorations on his chest. "I earned these in Korea. This is my National Defense Medal. This is my Bronze Star. This is my Purple Heart. I won't show you the scar—it's on my right leg—but I was one of the lucky ones. I don't even limp anymore."

"Mr. Demps, please."

"And this one, which you may not have seen before, is the Korean Service Medal. You may be interested to know that the blue and white in the ribbon are the colors of the United Nations. All free peoples, of all colors, united. And on the medal itself, see that? Here, let me hold it up to the light for you. That design is from the South Korean flag. It's called a *taegeuk*, and it's an ancient symbol, dating from the seventh century. It shows the yin and the yang, the opposites—low and high, light and dark, black *and* white— swirling together in harmony. How about that?"

Mr. Teale's voice was cold. "Mr. Demps, we thank you for your service in Korea, but it does not entitle you to a room at the Wakulla Springs Lodge. I'm afraid I must ask you to leave."

Jimmy Lee stepped back from the front desk and balled both hands into fists.

Behind the desk, Mr. Teale stepped back as well, and reached for the telephone.

Both the tennis men stood. One stepped toward Jimmy Lee.

Mr. Hubert picked up his waxer and ducked through the arched doorway to the enclosed porch, out of sight. Miss Carla had already disappeared.

And a three-foot alligator walked out from behind a potted palm, claws smacking wetly onto the tile, snout raised as if smelling the possibilities.

The tennis woman stood, took hold of a companion's arm— whether to cling to him or pull him back, Levi couldn't say—then saw the gator. She was closer to it than anyone else in the room. Her eyes widened. The cords in her neck stood out. Her mouth opened.

Levi was already at the foot of the stairs, clearing the last flight in two leaps.

The woman shrieked. "It's a monster!"

Levi ran across the lobby. He had no plan, exactly, but he hoped to put himself between the woman and the gator, the way Herbert A. Philbrick might have done. But he was only halfway across the lobby when the gator ran beneath the sofa. Without slowing, Levi changed course, skidded past the tennis woman, and jumped onto the sofa. The cushions were softer and deeper than he expected; he had to grab the back to keep from bouncing into the air.

The shrieking tennis woman was halfway across the lobby, her companions close behind her. Jimmy Lee ducked around them and ran for the sofa.

"Levi, don't move!" Jimmy Lee hollered. He picked up a free-standing ashtray and swung it before him like a club. Ashes and butts scattered across the tiles. "He's a little guy, but he could still take your hand off."

"I can flush him out," Levi said. He hopped up and down on the sofa.

"No, don't do that," Jimmy Lee said, but it was too late. The gator scuttled into view again, whipped its tail, and snapped its many teeth at the veteran.

"God almighty!" Mr. Teale cried.

Levi vaulted off the sofa, snatching up a pillow. He shook it at the gator, which whirled, darted forward and clamped it in his jaws. Levi let go, and the gator thrashed his head back and forth, shredding the pillow in a blizzard of feathers.

"Shoo!" Jimmy Lee told the gator. "Go that way. Outside. That way." He wasn't having much luck.

Strong hands gripped Levi's upper arms from behind. "Hang on, son," said an unfamiliar male voice. The next thing Levi knew, he was in midair, then behind the sofa. The stranger had just picked him up and set him down again out of harm's way, as easily as Jimmy Lee had picked up the ashtray. Levi turned. The man was big, more than six feet, very tan and broad-shouldered in a tight knit shirt, muscled legs bare beneath damp swim trunks.

"Come on, honey," the newcomer cooed at the gator. "Come on, now." He moved toward the gator in a crouch, arms spread wide. Jimmy Lee did the same from the other side, jabbing with the ashtray. Their unspoken mutual goal was to turn the gator, force it onto the enclosed porch, then outside. Instead the gator looked from one threat to the other, then dashed between them, across the lobby and through the archway leading to the ground-floor guest rooms.

Jimmy Lee and the newcomer said in unison, "Uh-oh." They ran to the archway, Levi right behind them.

Halfway down the otherwise deserted corridor, the gator saun-tered along the carpet, long head swinging from side to side, snout almost nudging each door in turn. At the far end was a closed exit door, its handle far out of the gator's reach.

"This isn't good," said the guy in the trunks. "Any ideas?"

"Not really," Jimmy Lee said. "But maybe we oughta bang on some doors, warn people to stay in their rooms?"

At that moment, the door alongside the gator opened, and a white-haired gentleman in a seersucker suit stepped out of Room 124 into the hallway, closing the door behind him with a snick, juggling too many small items in his hands: room key, pince-nez, pipe. The gator turned its head and regarded the old man with its cool prehistoric gaze. After interminable fumbling and muttering, the old man finally jammed the pince-nez onto his nose and stood motionless for a second, looking at the freshly revealed gator. He nodded and half-smiled, as he might have acknowledged a passing matron in the lobby, then turned and stepped back into Room 124, closing the door behind him just as gently as before. At the sound of the bolt being thrown, the gator was off again, scrambling down the corridor toward the far door.

Suddenly inspired, Levi turned and pounded back through the lobby—past a gasping Mr. Teale, who now knelt atop the front desk, a thin brass letter opener clutched in one scrawny hand— and through the main door, into the courtyard. He ran to the end of the brick walkway, flew around the corner to the outside door that led directly to the guest rooms, and flung it open, practically in the gator's face.

The gator stood there a moment, blinking in the sunlight.

Standing as clear of the doorway as he could, the boy held the door open as Jimmy Lee and the stranger in the swim trunks yelled and charged the gator from the far end of the corridor. It balked only an instant, then dashed for freedom, scrambling into the open air and heading across the parking lot, on a beeline for the little sinkhole in the woods opposite.

He would have made it, too, if a DeSoto Powermaster had not rounded the corner. The driver saw the gator just in time to yank the brakes. The DeSoto slewed sideways, raising dust, and a child in the back seat screamed, "Daddy, don't hit the dinosaur!" The gator reversed course, heading back the way he came. He was just past the doorway when the two men ran out. The gator made for the waterfront, and Levi ran behind it as Jimmy Lee and the swimmer fanned out to either side, waving their arms and yelling at the folks on the beach.

"Make way!"

"Let him through!"

"Here he comes!"

None of this, Levi thought, quite addressed the kernel of the situation, and the few tourists who had looked up just seemed confused, so he cupped both hands around his mouth and screamed, "GATOR!"

In a moment the waterfront was aboil. Swimmers and sunbathers leaped about like corn popping from a pan. Most of the swimmers thrashed toward the boathouse on one side, most of the sunbathers ran toward the diving platform on the other, and like Moses the gator steered unerringly for the part in the sea. It ran out of grass and launched itself across the beach, plowing a furrow in the sand to the water's edge. Suddenly graceful, hardly rippling the surface, the gator slid into Wakulla Springs, narrowed to a bumpy black sliver, and was gone. A few yards out, a drifting Donald Duck inner tube jerked, as if kicked from below, then began to slowly deflate. Levi stood on the beach between the soldier and the muscular stranger, all three out of breath, as they watched the now-tranquil water and listened to Donald's prolonged dying fart.

"What damn fool," Jimmy Lee finally asked, "let that gator into the hotel in the first place?"

"Um," the man in the swim trunks said. Jimmy Lee and Levi both stared at him. He glanced back, looking sheepish. "I thought he'd stay in the bathtub."

"You?" Jimmy Lee asked.

"You got me." He kept talking as they turned and walked back across the grass, toward the Lodge. "It was a dumb joke, a prank on one of our cameramen. He's had an alligator phobia, ever since he got to Florida. I swear he was afraid to get off the plane, thought they'd be waiting for him at the bottom of the gangway."

"How'd you catch it?" Levi asked, eyes wide.

The man laughed. "Catch it? Son, I bought it at a roadside stand, on the drive here." He spread his big hands and shrugged. "So yeah, the damn fool was me. I doubt if it'll be the last damn fool stunt I pull, either. Thanks for helping."

He held out his hand to Jimmy Lee, and after a pause only a Southerner could have registered, the soldier shook it.

"And thanks for your service," he added, nodding at the soldier's ribbons.

"You're welcome," Jimmy Lee said. He stopped walking, looking at the parking lot, and sighed. "Well, I'll be damned."

Mr. Teale had just set his suitcase and duffel bag on the curb.

Without looking up, the desk clerk walked briskly back inside, dusting his palms together. As he closed the glass door behind him, he flipped the hanging sign to read NO VACANCY.

"You could try again. I'd carry them back in for you," Levi said, surprising himself. "I'm pretty strong."

Jimmy Lee smiled, shook his head, squeezed Levi's shoulder. "We'll have plenty of chances, son," he said. "Right now, I think I need more help with your mom." To the swimmer, he said, "My name's Jimmy Lee Demps. My young friend here is Levi Williams."

The swimmer grinned as wide as the gator, his teeth almost too much for his mouth. "Pleased to meet you, Jimmy Lee. Levi," he said. "I'm Ricou Browning, the Beastie from the Black Lagoon."

<hr />

The monster's official name, in the daily flood of insignificant updates marked *urgent* from the studio in Hollywood—all delivered to the front desk of the Lodge by courier—was the Gill Man, but everyone on the Wakulla crew called it simply the Beastie.

At the moment, the Beastie was whining.

"Ouch!" Ricou cried.

"What a big baby you are." Winnie muttered around the clothespin clenched in her mouth. She gave the mesh skullcap an unnecessary yank. "If you'd just cut your hair, Mr. Handsome, you'd have an easier time of it. It sticks up like the Big Boy's. Bet you look good in those checked overalls."

Levi shinnied onto the riverbank to get a better look as the makeup woman tugged the skullcap over Ricou's unruly hair, then glued the back of the Beastie's head into place. To Levi, the companionable bickering of the two professionals was just one more element to admire. Levi no longer cared that Richard Carlson and the other credited stars of *Black Lagoon* would get no nearer

Wakulla Springs than the Universal lot in Hollywood, where all the "dry" scenes were being filmed. He had a new hero, and his name was Ricou Browning, this tall, handsome, goofy-grinned Florida State Seminole who wasn't just an athlete—he was a professional swimmer! Levi hadn't known there *were* professional swimmers.

And Ricou—he pronounced his name as in "Puerto Rico"—made his living right here in Florida! At the Weeki Wachee! With real mermaids! Sort of. That was what brought *Black Lagoon* to Levi's backyard: Mr. Newt Perry had worked at both places, and had recommended Wakulla and Ricou to Universal-International.

Ricou winced as some of the hot glue seeped through the mesh, burning him, and Levi grimaced in sympathy. Winnie had learned quickly enough not to overdo the glue in any one place, but accidents still happened.

Early each morning during the month-long shoot, Ricou had to sit at the water's edge in a form-fitting, head-to-toe leotard, while Winnie glued on the rubber Beastie suit piece by piece, one hand-sized fragment at a time. Latex, the rubber was called. By the second week, they had the process down to ninety minutes.

Until he absolutely had to leave or miss the school bus, Levi hovered about, bringing Ricou newspapers, butterscotch candies, whatever he needed, quizzing him and Winnie about everything they were doing, everything Scotty's camera unit was doing, everything Jim the Wakulla unit director was doing—which, Ricou maintained, wasn't much. All the underwater sequences had been storyboarded in Hollywood, which meant they had been drawn out frame by frame like a comic strip.

At first Levi had offered to bring Ricou drinks, but chugging orange juice in costume was a no-no. Ricou explained the studio had invested $18,000 in that suit—a fortune, far more than Levi's mama, than Winnie and Ricou, than anyone, really, earned in a year—and so Ricou was under strict orders not to pee in it.

Knowing this sort of thing made Levi very proud.

While working, Winnie chatted a lot about her friend Milicent, back at the studio. Milicent had designed the Beastie's face mask, although Winnie said Bud Westmore was taking most of the credit. "She told me the shape of the suit was inspired by the Oscar statue," Winnie said one morning.

"Huh," Ricou replied. "Well, that's as close to an Oscar as *this* picture's ever going to get." He winked at Winnie, and she swatted him with a glue rag. Winnie wore glasses, kept her red hair pinned back, and had freckles all over, at least as much as Levi could see. She and Ricou flirted a lot, when Levi wasn't interrupting.

One day Levi had asked: "If you came here because the water's so clear, why is the movie called *Black Lagoon*? Why aren't you shooting in dirty water someplace?"

Levi's new friends agreed that was a great question. While the cameramen *had* used the Lodge's boats to get some long tracking shots of the river's darker, swampier stretches, the underwater filming was all at the Springs because the water was crystal clear. "You're smarter than any studio executive," Ricou said, and Levi beamed.

Around the adults, Levi knew he was as much tolerated as welcomed, and he was desperate to show Ricou what he could really do. The chance came late one afternoon, after a long day's filming.

By then the waterlogged Beastie suit weighed a ton, and Ricou, exhausted, was unable to climb out of the water on his own. So he looped two nooses beneath his armpits and allowed himself to be hauled out by the same crane that raised and lowered the camera. Water pouring off him, looking like some deep-sea fisherman's nightmare catch, Ricou was swung ashore, where Winnie removed his mask and went to work on his chest plates.

"Hey!" Winnie poked Ricou in the side. "What happened here?"

He lifted his arms and craned his neck to look where she was poking, as if checking himself for ticks. "I'll be damned," he said, his catcher's-mitt paws reaching toward the sky in surrender. A triangular plate was missing, revealing the leotard beneath. "I knew that glue hadn't set up good. Hey, Scotty!" The frogmen on the far dock stopped fussing with their apparatus and looked toward Ricou, who gestured to his side and yelled, "You didn't film a piece of my hide coming off, did you?"

The frogmen conferred, all shaking their heads. "Not that we noticed," Scotty called back. "Where'd it go?"

"Beats me," Ricou muttered. He checked the ground beneath his feet, each fin flapping and cascading water as he lifted it. "Ah, hell. It must be in the river." Winnie knelt and raked her hands through the eelgrass along the shore.

"There it is!" Scotty cried.

Prompted by the cameraman's pointing finger, everyone looked far across the lagoon, where a bobbing bit of latex was moving steadily away from the Lodge on the current.

"Crackers," cursed Winnie. "There goes our left abdominal oblique."

"Hang on a sec," Scotty said. "Mitch is suiting up."

"No, I got it," Ricou called, instinctively turning to dive, but Winnie thrust the palm of her hand into his chest. The foam plates buckled inward with the pressure, spoiling the illusion of solid flesh.

"Nothing doing," said the makeup woman. "You're worn out, and we need to get these other pieces off you. We can't afford to lose any more, and you're shedding like a pinecone."

Ricou opened his mouth to protest, then held it open to gape as a small, lithe figure dashed past him and Winnie, diving headfirst into the lagoon.

Levi arrowed across the basin, just beneath the surface. He emerged only a few feet from the floating bit of latex. Hardly pausing to breathe, he plunged forward, grabbed the side-plate with both hands, brought his feet up beneath him and propelled himself backward toward the Lodge. Clutching the suit fragment to his chest like an otter, he swam with only mighty kicks of his feet. A few yards from shore he righted himself and stood, shaking his head and spraying water. He held the plate above his head like a diving trophy.

"I got it, Ricou! I got it!" Levi waded ashore, grinning, then froze as he realized what he had done. In public. He looked down at the off-limits, restricted water of Wakulla Springs sloshing around his ankles, then gaped at the all-white faces of the movie people. He turned toward the lodge, sure that he would see Mr. Ball himself standing there, hands on hips. Tomorrow Levi and his mama would be hitchhiking to Orlando.

But Mr. Ball wasn't there, only more movie people and, in the distance, some groundskeepers moving back and forth, paying Levi no attention at all.

"I'll take that," said Winnie, plucking the plate from the boy's hands and fanning it in the air to dry. "Thank you."

"Yeah, thanks," Ricou said. He shook his head in amazement. "Son, you are one fine swimmer. Anyone ever tell you that?"

"Everybody," Levi said, beaming. A safe distance out of the water now, he stared at Rico's claws and fins and segmented green suit. "Everybody tells me I'm half fish." On the make-up table, the Beastie's sightless, detached head stared at him in an unsettling way.

"Yeah, well," Ricou said. "Once Winnie peels off *my* half-fish, I want to see what you can do. How long can you hold your breath?"

"Three minutes."

"How deep you been?"

"Almost to the bottom. More than 100 feet, anyway. I like it down there. It's fun to look up at the sun."

"Hold still," Winnie said, kneeling beside Ricou. She used a putty knife to pry off each scaly segment and lay it in its numbered rack.

"Swim here a lot, do you?"

"Yep. All my life."

Winnie's knife paused. She looked up at Ricou. They both stared at Levi.

"Mostly at night," Levi added. "Nobody sees me."

"That's good," Winnie murmured, and went back to work.

"Hope you don't swim by yourself," Ricou said. "That's never a good idea, you know. At Weeki Wachee we never dive without a buddy." He flinched. "Ouch! Watch it, will you? I think some of me came off with the rubber that time." He turned back to Levi. "Hey, kid, you ever done any hose breathing?"

Levi solemnly shook his head.

Ricou smiled. "We'll just have to do something about that."

And so Levi the gofer became Levi the Beastie's apprentice.

Saturday morning, Levi breached the surface, spitting and coughing, water streaming from his eyes and nose. His throat burned.

He blinked until Ricou's head came into view, with its now-familiar curly hair, wide grin and ample nose. Ricou raised one clawed hand, latex webbing connecting the talons, and shook it at him. "OK, so what happened there?"

"I breathed through my nose—" Levi gasped.

"—and not through the hose," the two said together.

"That's right." Ricou nodded. "You know *here* that it's mouth breathing only," he said, tapping Levi's head with his claw, "but the message hasn't reached your lungs, when you're underwater and fighting for breath. The body takes longer to train. I was the same when Newt Perry taught me, at Weeki Wachee."

"I can do it, I know I can," Levi said. He pressed one nostril closed and blew snot out of the other, then reversed.

"The Beastie's head ready yet?" Ricou called.

"Hold your horses," yelled Winnie, yards away on the dock. Through the shoreline weeds, Ricou was visible to her, but not Levi. She knew the boy was there, all right, but no one on the film crew wanted to advertise the boy's presence when hotel guests might be around.

"Try it again?" Ricou asked.

"Sure," Levi said, and gave a thumbs-up that Ricou's rubber claw tried but failed to return. Levi took a deep breath, another and another, feeling the pleasant swell of his ribcage, then ducked beneath the water again.

The bubbling air hose lay on the shallow streambed at Levi's feet as he sat down, hanging on to a cypress root to keep from floating upward. Ricou talked a lot about the need to achieve "neutral buoyancy" instead of just gulping air until you filled up like a balloon, which confined you at or near the water's surface, but that was a lesson for another day. For now Levi was just counting seconds.

One Mississippi, two Mississippi. When he got to sixty Mississippi for the third time, he reached for the hose. He had trained himself to do it calmly, slowly, as if holding his breath for three minutes was the most natural thing in the world, and brought the end to his lips, the rushing bubbles tickling his face. With his free hand he pinched his nostrils shut, though he knew this was cheating. Fighting the artificial current, he wedged the hose between his lips, so that he had only a few drops of water to swallow, and inhaled with his mouth. He really did feel like a balloon this time, letting his lungs fill with air. Elated, he let go of the hose, allowing it to thrash itself back to the bottom like a snake, and after another minute, broke the surface, exhaling loudly as he did.

"Better," Ricou said.

"I did it!" Levi cried. "I did it!"

"You sure did," Ricou said, "and pretty soon you won't need to pinch your nose, either."

"How did you—oh." Levi had forgotten that Ricou could see him, even deep under the clear water.

"Calling all Beasties!" Winnie yelled.

Ricou waved one green paw. "I gotta go be a star now," he told Levi. "You keep practicing." He winked and walked away, finned feet flapping in the grass. He looked absurd above the water, just a man in a monster suit, but Levi watched him go with utter admiration.

Still elated by his triumph as a hose breather, Levi watched as Winnie secured the front of Ricou's mask. Seeing his friend slowly turn his head, looking at him with that strange froglike face, was eerie to the boy; he could believe Ricou had been transformed, right before his eyes, into something otherworldly and dangerous.

"We're ready when the Beastie is," Jim yelled across the springs. As usual during filming, he was sitting in an inner tube tethered to the diving platform, adrift over the water's depths. Scotty, the camera-crew chief, now strapping on the goggles of his frogman's suit and adjusting his aqualung, would give Ricou his cues below the surface. The underwater camera and its two-man crew were already in position, about fifty feet down.

"Ready or not, here he comes," Winnie said.

"Mmmmmph mmmmmph mrmm," Ricou said, and flipped backward into the water. He instantly became a different, graceful entity, cleaving the surface in an effortless backstroke, leaving a wake as perfectly V-shaped as a motorboat's. In the center of the lagoon, he righted himself, waited for the signal, then dropped from sight, like a man in a descending elevator. His mask held no breathing equipment, and the water closed over his head with scarcely a ripple.

"Gosh, he's good," murmured Winnie, hands on hips.

Scotty, goggles and breathing device in place, had years of experience on Ricou, but his drop into the water seemed, by comparison, as loud as a tourist boy's cannonball.

Levi slid into the water as noiselessly as he could, slipping across the river to the far side, hugging the bank, swimming just beneath the surface until he reached the place where he could dive deep. The springs were so clear that, even yards away, he could see Ricou getting his mimed cues from Scotty as the two camera operators treaded water beyond. The underwater camera was really two cameras bolted together, a necessity for the 3-D effect, with a frogman on each side pushing it forward.

Levi stuck close to the submerged cliff face, so he wouldn't get into the shot by accident.

Though filmed relatively early, in the movie this would be the Beastie's final scene. On Scotty's signal, Ricou went into his death throes, his supposedly bullet-riddled body pluming black-dye "blood" from multiple plastic packets as he burst them. His twitching slowed, and he began to sink. The frogmen angled the camera down to keep him in focus as he dropped farther and farther, webbed feet first, his arms seeming to float listlessly but actually gently sculling, propelling him toward the bottom of

Wakulla Springs, toward his next breaths of air, at the end of a bubbling hose held by another frogman. Levi watched until he thought
his own lungs would burst, and then he kicked toward the shore,
marveling that anyone could make death so graceful.

When darkness ended shooting for the day, Levi slipped into the
woods, put on his dry clothes, and walked home to the three-room
apartment in the employee dorm that he and his mother shared.
He wasn't surprised to find Jimmy Lee there, too. For the past
couple of weeks, the veteran was officially bunking with two of the
boatmen on the second floor, but he mainly used that as a place of
retreat whenever he and Levi's mama had a falling-out, which was
every couple of days. They weren't fighting now, though. Mama
was sprawled on the couch, in the fitful breeze of a slowly swiveling
table fan, drinking lemonade and reading a book called *The Day of
the Locust*. Tourists brought books on vacation then just left them
behind, so Mama always had something to read on her day off.

"And here he is," murmured Jimmy Lee. He sat in a chair, leafing
through a stack of mail, as usual, all of it politics. Jimmy Lee Demps
got more mail every day than the Lodge itself.

"Hi, baby," his mama said.

"Hey," said Levi, pushing his head into his mama's neck for the
obligatory hug. She squeezed him even harder than usual, then
held him at arm's length for inspection.

"You been bothering those movie people again?" she asked.

"Ricou's teaching me to breathe through a hose underwater,"
Levi said, "just like the swimmers at the Weeki Wachee."

His mother shook her head and sighed. "Honey, they don't need
no colored mermaids at the Weeki Wachee. You got to get your
mind back on school. Ain't that right, Jimmy Lee?"

"Mmm," said Jimmy Lee. He opened an envelope and slid out a bumper sticker that said, DON'T BUY GAS WHERE YOU CAN'T USE THE REST ROOM.

What good was a bumper sticker, Levi wondered, when you ain't got a bumper, or a car neither?

Jimmy Lee winked at Levi and nudged Mayola in the ribs, trying to show her the sticker. "We ought to go to this Negro Leadership rally one year, baby. It's really something."

"I got another note from your teacher," Levi's mama said. She put her book down and gave him her full-on attention.

Levi gulped. Mama was always going on and on about school, like it was holy as church, but she looked fearsome serious this time.

"*Day*dreaming," she continued with emphasis. "Falling asleep in class. Levi, I know it's exciting, your very own monster movie right here at the springs, and I'm trying to be patient. There ain't much for a growing boy hereabouts, I know that. But if you really want to get out of this place one day, you gotta concentrate on your studies."

Levi nodded, but said nothing.

His mama took a long, slow drink of lemonade, without taking her eyes off him. "So here's how it's gonna be. If I get one more note about your sorry-ass ways, young man, you won't be dipping a single toe into *any* kind of water 'cept a bathtub till you're a bent-over, white-haired old man. You hear me?"

"But Mama," Levi said. "I got to keep swimming. Ricou says people can make a good living at it. Cameras are getting smaller, so lots more movie crews'll be coming to Florida, and they'll hire locals to help. Ricou's thinking about starting his own business."

His mama put her book down onto the couch cushion and rubbed her temples. "Levi, you listen up, and you listen good. How many times I got to tell you, you can't trust movie people?"

She winced, squeezing her eyes shut. "They charm you," she murmured, "and they tell you how great you are, and they make you feel like you're something—special, real special. But then they go and pack right up and leave." She rubbed her head again. "It's just play-acting, Levi. Our lives ain't anything to them." She groaned. "Oh, Lord, I feel another headache coming on. Jimmy Lee, please do turn off that lamp."

"I'll fetch you a potato," Levi said. As he ran to their kitchenette, he felt relieved to escape from the whole subject of school, but ashamed at his relief. As he grabbed a good-sized spud and sliced it into discs, he wondered why every conversation with his mama, these days, made him feel guilty. Was that what growing up was all about?

"A potato," he heard Jimmy Lee repeat.

"To lay on my forehead," his mama said softly.

Jimmy Lee laughed, but he cut it off quick—Mama probably gave him one of her looks.

"It always helps," Levi said, returning with a saucer of potato slices. He set them down at her elbow.

"Bring Mama a handkerchief, too, baby." She had her arm across her eyes now.

"Yes'm," Levi said.

"No, here," Jimmy Lee smiled. "Allow me." He plucked a bright red handkerchief from his pants pocket and offered it with a small flourish, as if it were a bouquet of roses.

Levi's mama raised her forearm just enough to glance at the handkerchief through slitted eyes. "That won't work," she said, listlessly and automatically. She closed her eyes again. "Levi, honey, bring me one from the dresser, please."

"What's wrong with this one?" Jimmy Lee asked, still holding it out.

"It has to be white," Levi said, and regretted it instantly. He stood there, his mama lay there, and Jimmy Lee sat there, all of them seemingly frozen in place.

"White," Jimmy Lee repeated. His voice was quiet, but a vein in his temple stood out and, without thinking, Levi backed away, hitting the washstand, which tilted and rattled but didn't fall.

"If the handkerchief ain't white," Levi's mama murmured, "the healing won't work. That's what the root doctor say."

"Is it?" Jimmy Lee's voice was even more quiet, and Levi's mama opened her eyes. She frowned and slowly raised her head just enough to see him.

"Jimmy Lee?"

He was already at the door, his rejected handkerchief puddled on the floor where he had dashed it down.

"Jimmy Lee, for heaven's sake."

The door slammed and the framed cameo of Levi's great-grandfather in American Expeditionary Forces uniform danced against the plaster wall, *tap tap, tap tap.*

Levi's mama burst into tears.

"Don't, Mama, please don't," Levi said. "Here, see? I got your potatoes, there they are—don't that feel better? Lemme get that handkerchief, you hang on, just don't cry. Please, Mama. Levi's here. Don't cry, Mama. It's you and me, just like always."

━━━━━━

When his mama finally got to sleep, Levi went for a ramble in the woods.

He went down to the riverbank and walked along the south shore of the Wakulla for a few hundred yards. He stopped to listen to every rustle, every crackle, every slither, every *thud* of something dropping from the trees into the mulch of the forest floor, every *plop* of something long and heavy sliding into the water, and especially every chilling wail of the limpkin:

Kw-E-E-E-E-E-E-ah!

Familiar as it was, the limpkin's nighttime cry always seemed weird—alien too. It raised goosebumps on Levi's arms. Although if he turned his head, he could see the boathouse, the bathhouse, and the water fountains, only a few minutes' walk upstream, as he stood in a pitch-black thicket, watching the dark streaks of gators crossing the moonlight on the surface of the river, Levi could easily imagine that he was in some faraway jungle. Left to his own devices, he would creep through the woods every night, listening for monsters.

Florida was chock full of them; all the old-timers said so. Employees at Wakulla Springs came from all over the state, and brought their stories with them. The men who had hung out in the St. Marks bait shacks talked about Old Hitler, the thousand-pound hammerhead that cruised north from Tampa Bay to torment fishermen by shredding the lines, eating the day's catch, and butting holes in the boat. They said the shark was more than a hundred years old—how else could it have grown so big, and as smart as a man? Levi believed every word, but wondered what it had been called before the Nazis came along.

People who lived at the mouth of the Apalachicola said a snakelike thing lived in the river. Bigger around than a cypress trunk, the creature swam against the current like an inchworm, each stinking mossy hump rising so far above the surface that it once splintered beams on the John Gorrie Bridge.

Howard, the pantry chef, hunted coons in Tate's Hell Swamp. Several of his friends had staggered out, swearing their missing dogs had been taken by black panthers that lay silently along high oak branches, motionless and drowsy, until scenting the hounds—and the men, for which they had acquired a taste, during the Civil War.

And everybody in Florida talked about the wilderness-dwelling Skunk Ape. Taller than a man, it shambled along on its knuckles, reeking of sour cabbage, harrumphing deep in its chest, *woomp*, *woomp*.

Levi believed in all of those creatures, believed in them utterly and completely, because they had been seen and described and attested to a hundred times over by grown-ups, and because he was half-convinced that he had seen and heard them on his own walks. Every night, it seemed, he heard and saw things even stranger and more awful—and therefore better—along the whir-ring chirping grunting splashing midnight shore of the Wakulla River, which he knew as well as any gator.

Besides, who would want to grow up and live in a world where every living critter was known and explained and catalogued, or penned up in a zoo or alligator farm or serpentarium? Levi was even willing to believe in the Clearwater Monster, which had famously churned up the sand a few years back and been declared by experts as something like a giant penguin, even though a giant penguin in Florida seemed a lot less likely than even a Skunk Ape. Levi's mother said anyone who would believe in a giant penguin waddling down Clearwater beach was dumb as limestone and probably jake-leg drunk to boot. But Levi still believed.

On this night, Levi stared at the moonlit river more intently than usual, almost desperate for something out of the ordinary to hap-pen, and was eventually rewarded when a big black shape glided past, accompanied by a repeated *plunk* like water being displaced by a paddle. For a moment, Levi was certain it was the phantom Indian brave that the Seminoles believed patrolled the river at night in his stone canoe, keeping the waters clear and the air free of evil spirits, then realized it was Old Joe. Eleven feet long, the springs' most famous alligator played second fiddle to no dead Indian. The *plunk* was Old Joe's massive tail cleaving the water as he swam. Levi fancied that Old Joe looked his way as he passed, one river creature acknowledging another, but who could say for sure? Late at night along the mysterious Wakulla, all certainty flowed eastward with the current, as Old Joe's sidewinder motions sent little waves lapping over Levi's toes, and the limpkins' screams pierced the silence of the woods, and something aways off went *woomp, woomp.*

It took Levi more than an hour to make his way back to the dormitory. Past his bedtime. The lights in their apartment were off, and he kept his shoes in his hands as he swung his legs over the railing and padded across the porch, hoping to slip inside the door without disturbing his mama. But he heard low voices as he approached, and instinct made him stop and listen. His mama and Jimmy Lee were talking in the dark. Levi couldn't quite make out their words until he crept along the stucco wall to a spot by the azaleas, beneath her bedroom window. He smelled cigarette smoke, and heard the *tink* of a bottle against a drinking glass.

"Hold up, there," his mama said. "I've had enough already."

"I'll be the judge of that," said Jimmy Lee, laughing.

Nobody spoke for a while, though Levi heard something rustle, and his mama actually giggled.

How was it that grown-ups could have knock-down-drag-out fights one minute, and be snuggling and kissing the next? Levi sometimes thought that adults must make up their moods randomly as they went along.

"Jimmy Lee, wait. Wait, I said. Not now."

"Why not now?"

"Because now I need to tell you some things I did years ago. Two things."

"You don't have to tell me anything."

"Yes, I do."

"No, baby. I already know about the white man."

Levi held his breath.

She laughed, an odd laugh, like that was funny and sad at the same time. "He's always 'the white man' to you. He was a man. Ain't that enough?"

Jimmy Lee said, after a moment. "You're right. That is enough. But I know about it, and it doesn't matter to me anymore."

"I'm glad. But that's not what I need to tell you. It's about after. After I knew I was—pregnant."

"With Levi."

"Yes, with Levi. Who else I been pregnant with?"

"I'm sorry. I guess I just needed to talk. I'll hush."

"Hush, then. Let me tell it, so that I can say *why* I need to tell you."

"Yes ma'am."

"I knew, and my mama knew, but no one else. It was early. I mean, I didn't show. But I was sick every morning. Lord, what sickness! I haven't touched okra since. I was really just a child myself, and scared to death."

"So the father didn't know?"

"*Never* knew. Like I told you before. You just gonna have to take my word that was impossible." A rustle. "Besides, I thought you were going to hush."

"All right. I'm hushing. You were scared."

"Scared, and wanted a way out. Wanted the baby to go away and leave me alone, have him go get born to somebody else and give me my old life back."

"Him?"

"What?"

"You said *him*."

"Yes. Somehow I knew, even then, it was a boy. Lucky guess." She cleared her throat, and Levi heard ice rattle in a glass. "Lucky? Hmm. Anyway, I asked my mama how that would work, how I could end it. Lord, she had a blue fit. 'Child, that is murder,' she said. 'That is the original sin, to kill your own kin. Get down on the floor with me right now.' So we prayed on it for an hour, there on the kitchen floor. Well, she prayed, anyway, asking God to forgive my childish thoughts. I just lay on my side, wrapped around her knees, crying. Picked up a splinter in my cheek, see? Right there. So when she was prayed out and I was cried out, she got me up and hugged me, then got her tweezers and tried to work out the splinter, which didn't go so well, 'cause I kept flinching and crying, and finally she set down the tweezers and reached up with her fingernails and plucked it out, just like that. I didn't feel a thing. That was the last I ever said about getting rid of the baby. Except one time."

The ice rattled again in the glass, and Levi heard his mama blow out air, *pluuuuuuuuh*, and he knew she was passing the cold wet glass across her forehead, like she always did when it was hot and she was stalling for time. Jimmy Lee said nothing, and finally Mama started up again.

"See, Old Mr. Gavin up and died, if you can *up* and do anything when you're ninety-one, and we went to the lying-in. Mr. Gavin was related to every colored person between Mobile and Tampa, so Mama and I had to stand in line to pay our respects. I was standing there crying—I cried at the drop of a hat, in those days—not feeling sorry for Mr. Gavin, just sorry for myself, when I remembered a funny old tale Mr. Gavin told me once, when I had the chicken pox. He said one way to cure a sickness is to whisper into a dead person's ear."

"To do *what*?" Jimmy Lee's voice got louder.

"I *wondered* if you was paying attention."

"I never heard tell of *that*. What are you supposed to whisper?"

"You whisper the dead person's name, and then you ask the dead person, real nice, whether he'd be willing to take your sickness away with him. It won't hurt him, after all. He's already dead."

"My God."

"Anyway, right about that time the woman who was blubbering over the casket finally got done, so Mama and I moved up in line, and she reached down and patted Mr. Gavin's wrinkly bald head, and kissed his cheek, and moved on to say hey to some of the Pensacola people. And even though I knew it was just some old wives' tale, before I could change my mind I leaned down close to Mr. Gavin's ear—they say your ears keep growing all your life, and that must be true, because Mr. Gavin's ear was the size of a cabbage leaf, folded across half his head, and what was even stranger was there was no heat at all, not like you feel when you're that close to a living person—and I whispered 'Mr. 'Lonzo Gavin, this is Mayola Williams, and please won't you think about taking this baby with you when you go, thank you kindly.' Then I stood up, and someone asked me to tote a plate of chicken out to the porch, and it was over. I'd done it."

"No one heard you?"

"Jimmy Lee, Mr. *Gavin* couldn't hear me, him being dead and me whispering so low and fast. Wasn't really a whisper, more like a breath with a thought inside it. But that thought was there. And when I come through the house with the plate, even though it was a gracious amount of chicken, I felt lighter than I had in weeks, almost bouncing when I walked, and I knew—I mean, I just *knew*—that Mr. Gavin had taken my baby with him. But he hadn't. Six months later, Levi was born, and to this day, every night when

I stand in his doorway and watch him sleep, I thank God and Mr. Gavin that neither one of them heard what I whispered—and that Mama didn't hear it neither."

"Why tell me now?"

"Because I want you to stop throwing off on superstitions. If I tell you I don't have a headache anymore when I take the sliced potatoes off my forehead, I want you to say you're glad of that. A thing that comes down to you because whole generations told it to each other, before you ever showed up, that deserves respect whether you believe it or not. Now, maybe I didn't half believe what Mr. Gavin had told me, and I still don't, but I know I *wanted* it to be true, and I know that the doing of it gave me a lightness."

"But, Mayola—"

"Hush. I also know I'm damn lucky it didn't work that time, because luck has a way of coming—or not—that is beyond any of our knowing or doing and you can't convince me otherwise."

"All right." Jimmy Lee was quiet for a minute before he said, "You said there was two things?"

"Yes. Well, the second thing—" Levi heard the clink of ice and a splash of something wet and a *long* bit of quiet before he heard his mama's voice again. "The second thing I ain't never told another living soul before. Not my mama, for sure. Not even Vergie."

"I'm listening."

More quiet. Then she said, "He gave me money."

"Who did?"

"The man."

"I thought you said he didn't know?"

"He didn't." Levi heard another *pluuuuh* of blown-out air, another stall. "He gave it to me—before."

"*What?*" Jimmy Lee's voice was loud again, and now it had iron in it.

"He gave me a hundred dollars. He was rich and it wasn't nothing but pocket money to him. And that's what I used for the doctor when Levi was born." Levi felt his stomach turn over like he'd eaten too many biscuits all at once. He heard the bedsprings squeak. "There, Jimmy Lee. I've said it."

"Yes, you sure have. Why? Why now?"

"Because if you and me are gonna have a life together, and maybe have a child of our own, I don't want no secrets between us. I needed you to know every single thing, and now you do."

If Jimmy Lee said anything in reply, Levi didn't hear it. He was already running across the dew-wet lawn and back into the woods, where even the wisteria seemed to know to get out of his way.

He used to run like this imagining the TV narrator in his head: *This is the fantastically true story of Herbert A. Philbrick, who for nine frightening years led three lives—average citizen, member of the Communist Party, and counterspy for the FBI.* But that suddenly seemed very childish.

He ran full out until he reached the little hidden sink nearest the Lodge. Ignoring the grunting bullfrog that on any other night he would have stalked and observed, he sat down and thought about what he had heard, though much of it was hard to think about, literally: It would not hold his concentration.

The part that he could let through came in a steady beat like the bullfrog's mating call:

The doorway.

She stands in the doorway and watches me when I sleep.

Why did she never tell me that? Why did I never know?

He sat there a long time thinking, not really listening to the bullfrog or the other night-plopping creatures until the breathy singsong of someone sauntering up the Lodge driveway made it into his ears—

Numbers, numbers, 'bout to drive me mad
Numbers, numbers, 'bout to drive me mad
Thinking 'bout the money that I should have had

The voice was heading away from the building and out toward the road when Levi suddenly stirred himself, fisted away the tears he didn't remember crying, and stepped through the trees and into the drive directly in front of Policy Sam, who jumped a foot into the air with a yelp.

"Hey, Sam."

"Damn, Levi! I thought the Skunk Ape done got me. If I'd'a dropped these tickets, I'd have played hell picking them up, too."

"You going to Cooper's?" Levi asked.

"Yeah, I'm going to the Big House. Got a late toss tonight."

"Can I go with you?"

If Sam had asked, "Why?" Levi would have been stuck for an answer. All he knew was that he suddenly didn't want to be alone any more, but he didn't want to go home, either; if he saw his mama now, he would bust out crying, just like a baby—*an unwanted baby* was the thought he couldn't let himself think, nor about another baby that his mama might want. That overheard conversation had set so many grown-up thoughts to swimming through his head that he needed to *do* something grown-up, this very night.

But Sam didn't say a word.

"Look, I just want to see what it's like. You been asking me to go with you, right?"

"Sure I have," Sam said, though he didn't sound so sure.

"Well, let's go. I'll buy a number if that's what it takes," Levi said. "How about ninety-one?" It was the first number that came to mind: Mr. Gavin's age when he died. He'd never even heard of Mr. Gavin before.

"Ninety-one? Numbers only go up to seventy-eight."

"Oh. Well, seventy-eight, then." Levi pulled some coins out of his pocket.

Sam hesitated, but finally handed over a single strip of paper. "Okay, then, come along. But you best pick 'em up and put 'em down, 'cause we got to hustle out to the county road and I'm running late already. The men drinking down at the boats was trying to count lightning bugs, and that is one slow-ass way of picking numbers." He shook his head. "Levi Williams, playing the numbers. Never thought I'd see it. Ain't you scared of your mama no more?

"I ain't studying about her," Levi said, and then walked in silence, because in fact she was all he *was* studying about, all down the long drive and out to the paved road, the cracked white paint of the center line seeming to glow like a ghost trail leading off into the darkness.

Policy Sam stopped by the side of the road heading south.

"What're we waiting for?" Levi asked.

"Henry. On late-toss nights, him and me got an arrangement."

Levi was about to ask who Henry was when a battered taxi tooted its horn and pulled off onto the shoulder, motor running.

"C'mon," Sam said. He tugged Levi across the pavement and opened the back door. "Hey, Henry." He slid in, and Levi followed.

"Well, well, well. If it ain't swimming boy."

Levi was startled until he noticed the man's white stubbled hair and the pictures of Lena Horne on the dashboard.

"That soldier with the big ideas, he still keeping company with your mama?"

"Yessir," Levi said, to be polite, then slumped way down into the cracked leather seat to put an end to any further conversation.

"Thirty-nine and forty-two," Sam said, peeling off two strips of paper from the bundle in his fist. "There you go." He handed them over the seat. Henry pocketed them and grunted, then put the car into gear.

It was eight miles from the springs to the county seat at Crawfordville. More than two hours walking—and that was *fast* walking the whole way—but Henry pulled the cab to a stop in front of Cooper's no more than twenty minutes later.

〰〰〰〰〰

Levi had heard talk about Cooper's his whole life, in dribs and drabs of conversations he was not supposed to have any part of—listening to Aunt Vergie and the rest of the crew tell tales, especially after a weekend, when lots of folks seemed to get headaches and have shorter tempers than usual. He had imagined it to be a grand palace, a party that never stopped, with the bright lights and music that signified grown-up fun.

But when he got out of Henry's cab, his first thought was that it ought to be called the Chicken House instead of the Big House. It was a long, low, swaybacked building with double doors on either end, built of concrete blocks, sallow light escaping through square chicken-wire windows every few feet. Sam and Levi joined the stream of people jostling into the south door. People added themselves on from all directions in ones, twos, and threes, men and women, mostly colored but some whites and Cubans as well, and of course plenty of boys, running in last-minute numbers.

Levi was shorter by a head than most of the crowd. After a minute he couldn't see anything but the back of Sam, and he held on tight to the tail of the other boy's shirt, half-suffocated and half-crushed by the time they finally pushed their way inside. Some palace. A battered tin-top bar ran the length of the east wall. The scattered furnishings were all mismatched: orange crates, card tables, upturned buckets and barrels, funeral-home chairs, anything you could sit on or set a beer on. Off in a corner, a scratchy nickel phonograph was playing Nat King Cole and scores of people just stood around, talking, laughing, whooping.

Runners stood in line before a desk in the corner, where a fat colored man gnawed the butt of a cigar as he collected stacks of coins and wadded bills. A skinny colored woman sat beside him with a pencil and a thick notebook. His voice loud to be heard over the crowd, Sam said she was recording the numbers sold that day: how many of each, and who bought them. He pointed to a quiet spot along the west wall and told Levi to stay put until *he* was done with his business.

Levi watched, hands in his pockets, afraid to look at anything but Sam as he made his way through the runners' line. Occasionally the fat man and the skinny woman turned from their counting and writing to whisper into each other's ears, and once, Levi was startled to see them kiss on the lips.

When the runners left the desk, they simply threw down their unsold numbers. Discarded paper strips covered the Big House floor, forming ankle-deep drifts along the walls. Walking in here meant wading through numbers.

Men all around Levi were betting on everything: how many drinks would be on Mae's tray when she left the bar; how many more runners would come in the door at the last minute; who in the group had the biggest knife in his pocket.

Levi was less interested in Mae's glass-laden tray than in the shortness of her skirt. He got a very good look as she passed by, because she slowed down and brushed nearer him than was strictly necessary.

"How old are you, baby?" she asked him. She had a big mole on her right cheek, and a gap in her front teeth that a gar could swim through. Levi couldn't make his tongue answer.

"Older'n he was when he come in," a big man laughed.

"Ain't that right," another man added. "And if you keep rubbing against him he'll get bigger yet."

"Screw you," Mae said, and the men roared like that was the wittiest thing ever said.

When Sam finally reached the desk, the fat man and the skinny woman performed the necessary transactions and paid him no more attention than they did anyone else. But Sam walked over to Levi, jingling change in his pockets, beaming at everyone as if he owned the place. "Some party, huh?" Sam asked. They leaned side by side against the wall, watching the crush. "Line's about done. They'll do the toss in fifteen, twenty minutes."

Levi kicked at the ruck of slips on the floor. "Do they throw these away later?"

Sam laughed. "Like hell. Don't you know it's bad luck to throw away a Policy number? Or burn one, or tear it up? Makes that number bad for you and bad for everybody else, too. No, you got to bury them, so your luck keeps growing."

Levi nearly said something about how country ignorant that was, but then he remembered what his mama had told Jimmy Lee about respecting superstitions, and he held his tongue and thought of a more practical objection.

"Look, Sam, right there at my toe, face up, is a five, lying there as pretty as you please. Now, I bought a seventy-eight, not a five. But if a five gets drawn, what's to keep me from throwing mine down, picking that up and hollering, 'I got a five, I'm a winner'?"

"Maybe nothing," Sam replied, smiling in a way that made Levi's neck prickle. "Pick it up and see."

Levi hesitated, because he didn't like the look in Sam's eye, but he leaned over and picked up the five—then couldn't straighten up. One powerful hand gripped his forearm; another clamped the back of his neck. He feared he could feel his bones grinding together in each spot.

"Drop it," said a man's voice, "or I break your arm."

"It's dropped!" Levi said, and it was. A patent-leathered foot kicked through the numbers, burying the five, and both hands let go of Levi. Dizzy with terror, he slumped against the wall to steady himself and looked around for his assailants. He saw only the same crush of betting men, several of whom looked strong enough, but no one paid him the slightest attention, now that he wasn't stealing a number.

"You see how it is?" said Sam.

"I sure do," Levi said, rubbing his arms. "Anyone standing beside me could be working for the house. Spies everywhere."

Sam laughed. "You dummy, the house don't need no spies. Any customer in the place would kill a cheater soon as look at him. You walk out honest, or you don't walk out. You want a Nehi?" He turned and scanned the crowd. "Hey, Jo!"

A waitress shifted her tray and looked down. "Hey, Sam."

"You got any Blue Cream?"

"No Blue Cream, sugar," she said. Her skirt was even shorter than Mae's. Jo wasn't much older than the boys, but she loomed over them; her chest was about level with Sam's eyes. A small scar descended from her left eye like a tear. "Got Orange, Peach, Ginger, and a few Wild Berry left. They're warm. Nobody gonna leave for ice and miss the toss."

"I *like* my Nehi hot," Sam said, winking at her, "but Orange is for crackers. Gimme a Wild Berry." Looking bored, she held her hand out, palm up, and he dropped coins into it. "One for my buddy, too," Sam said, "and keep the change."

"My fortune is made," she drawled. She turned to Levi, who had finally registered her high heels. No wonder she was so tall: She was practically on tiptoe. "You want a Wild Berry, too?"

"No, ma'am. Orange is fine," Levi squeaked, his voice cracking. "How do you walk on those things?"

She grinned. "Like this." She turned and sashayed away, demonstrating.

Levi gaped.

Sam's elbow jabbed him. "See what you been missing?" Sam was only a year older than him, but Levi could tell he was right at home here. "Ain't this great?" Sam hollered.

Even face-to-face conversation had to be hollered now, over the crowd and the din. All the men were sweaty, and all smoking. The top half of the room was a pungent gray haze, and Levi was glad to be below it.

A nearby group of men roared with laughter over something, and one of them smashed a bottle against the wall for emphasis. Another yelled, "If that ain't a show, I'll kiss your ass!"

Sam pulled him over to one of the windows. "They'll draw a nine tonight," he said.

"How do you know?"

"I dreamed about a wild hog last night. It was ruttin' in the back parlor of my grandma's house, and no one paid it any mind, like only I could see it. Then it caught me lookin' and chased me out of the house. A crazy kind of dream. The Black and White Luck Book says when you dream about wild animals, you should play a five, a seven, or a nine, and they already drew five and seven this week. Hey, there, baby."

Jo sashayed back into view, their Nehis on a tray. Someone already had popped the caps, and the drinks were flat on top of being warm, but Levi gulped his, feeling the sweet syrup gurgling inside his chest as Jo looked him up and down. A thought came into Levi's head, one that he'd give anything to chase back out. *Was my mama like these girls?*

Jo opened her mouth and said something else, but the room had erupted in such a roar that Levi didn't hear a word of it. Everyone cheered as the middle of the room cleared to make room for the fat man and the skinny woman. She carried a tray of numbered balls, the man a croker sack.

Levi frowned at Jo and cupped his ear, miming, "What?" She leaned forward, said something else that Levi lost entirely, then reached up to his chest and twisted his left nipple, right through his shirt, winking as she did. He cried out in pain and surprise. Then she turned and slipped into the crowd, disappearing as completely as an envelope through the mail drop at the Lodge. Levi turned to Sam—for help or confirmation or he didn't even know what—but Sam had eyes only for the couple in the middle of the room.

"Ladies and gentlemen!" squawked the fat man. "May I direct your attention to my lovely assistant's tray, featuring balls numbered one to seventy-eight. Please take a moment, you folks standing closest, to confirm that each number is fairly represented."

A dozen people leaned forward to look, nodding their heads.

"And please note, you folks nearest me, that my sack is entirely empty." He made a big show of turning it inside out and back again, stretching the neck wide for all to see. Then he held it out to the skinny woman, who tipped her tray and poured the numbered balls into the sack. The fat man swiftly tied the neck of the sack into a knot, then stepped a few feet away and threw the bulging sack to the woman. She threw it back to him, and the back-and-forth continued, across a wider and wider space. The crowd surged closer, everyone shouting their favorite numbers at the tops of their lungs.

Levi had had enough of the noise, the heat, the smoke, the greed. He dropped his empty Nehi bottle, feeling sick to his stomach. His nipple ached, and he half dreaded—although a small, unfamiliar part of him also half hoped—that the scarred waitress would reappear at any moment on her teetering deer's legs to claim him. "I'm gonna go," he said to Sam, who was oblivious.

Hugging the wall, unnoticed, Levi sidled toward the exit as fast as the crowd would let him. He stumbled alone into the cool night air, around the building and into the clean freshness of the piney woods that stretched, unbroken, for seventy miles west from Crawfordville.

The Apalachicola National Forest, the largest in the state of Florida. His teacher said it was almost a thousand square miles, most of it unexplored swampy wilderness, the kind a person could get lost in, never to be seen again. The idea was not without its appeal, right then.

Levi walked in a ways, far enough that the noise of Cooper's was just a drone, no louder than the cicadas and the frogs, found an old loblolly pine stump, and sat down to breathe the stink out of his lungs and gather his thoughts.

But his thoughts all bounced around between Jo and Mae and his mama and Jimmy Lee and the white man—whoever he was— that was his daddy, and suddenly Levi was doubled over, vomiting a stream of warm Orange Nehi. When he was emptied out, his throat raw and sour, he took three chest-spreading breaths, as if he had just returned to the surface after a long, deep dive.

He wiped his mouth with his shirttail and started to sit again when he heard a thump, somewhere off in the darkness behind him and then another, off to his right. Levi vomited again, though this time nothing came up but thin bile.

When they learned about the Apalachicola woods in class, a

boy named Emmit said that he knew for gospel that a wild creature lived in the swamps far back into this forest, hair all over his body, bigger even than a Skunk Ape. It smelled of rotting meat and howled when it was hungry—for human blood. Emmit was dumber than a bag of hammers, but his daddy was a hunter, and knew as much about this part of the world as any man, so Levi thought there was likely some truth to the tale.

After what he'd seen and heard tonight, he didn't know what he believed any more.

Levi began to walk back toward the road when, deep in the darkness far behind him, something howled, long and low, raising every hair on Levi's body and putting his feet in a mood for some serious running.

He crashed through the underbrush, feeling a tug on his shirt, then a ripping sound, but he didn't care about his clothes, not one bit. He ran faster, his sneakers crunching over twigs and stirring up leaves, making enough noise to scare the devil himself—he hoped—and headed for the lighted bulk of Cooper's Big House.

He finally stumbled around the corner, and leaped back just in time to avoid being splattered by a fat man pissing against the cinderblocks.

"Well, hey there, Jackie Robinson," said Henry the taxicab driver, zipping up. "You a runner too, now?"

"Nossir." Levi gulped air, trying to loosen up a stitch in his side. "Can you take me home?" He'd had enough of the grown-up world and wanted to be back in his own bed more than anything he could remember wanting. "Please?" He heard his voice crack with the pleading.

"Sorry, son," the cabbie said. "I got paying fares leaving this joint for the next three hours, going all over the county. But it's a nice night for a walk, a strong boy like you."

"Yessir," Levi said, his shoulders sagging. "Thanks anyway."

As Levi walked home, keeping to the shoulder of the road and the edge of the woods, he slowly tore his number seventy-eight into tiny pieces that he dropped behind him like a trail of bread-crumbs in a story. Bad luck? Maybe. But the farther he got from Cooper's, the luckier he felt.

〰〰〰〰〰

The sun was barely above the horizon when Levi trudged up the long winding driveway. Almost home. At the Springs, at least. Home was where he'd catch holy hell, but not just yet. He cut into the woods and walked straight to the lagoon, shedding clothes as he went, some of the Big House stink falling behind with each piece. He emerged a few yards from the diving tower.

That was where he had always stopped, as a child, at the edge of the swimming area restricted to tourists, where water creatures that looked like him were forbidden. But in the dawn of a new day, Levi Williams stood on the grass, naked as the day he was born, and fear of Mr. Ball and his laws—or his mama and her rules—fell away like the dried-up used skin of a canebrake rattler.

He put one foot onto the concrete steps of the tower, then another, and then he was climbing up and around and up again until he stood at the very edge of the topmost platform, thirty feet above the springs. Levi stopped there, watching the pale light play across the surface of the water, feeling a little ball of fierceness grow inside him. This was *his* water, as much as anyone's.

Levi took a deep breath—one, two, three—and launched him-self into space, diving hands-first into the deepest part of Wakulla Springs. Water roaring in his ears, he plunged twenty, thirty feet down, thirty-five, until his natural buoyancy took over and he began to rise again. The exhaustion of a long night disappeared and he pushed the water behind him with easy strokes, propelling himself forward, a school of gar disintegrating in a thousand directions as he swam through it.

He swam underwater, coming up for air at two-minute intervals, moving to the far side of the lagoon, unnoticed by the film crew beginning to set up for the day's shoot. His head barely breaking the surface, Levi watched from afar as Winnie encrusted Ricou's long, lean body with Beastie scales. He watched from afar as Ricou joked with her and with a blonde Weeki Watchee girl, a stunt double in a high-cut white swimsuit, who donned a black wig just before she jumped into the water. He watched from afar as the crew lowered the camera into place, as Ricou and the stand-in lazily swam into position.

Then: Action.

Levi dived deep again, down to a rock ledge, holding on with his toes, and looked up. Silhouetted against the sun, the girl in the white swimsuit swam on the surface. Beneath her swam the Beastie, mirroring her movements. And now beyond them—unseen by either swimmers or cameras—swam Levi, matching Ricou kick for kick, stroke for stroke.

When the girl straightened, rested one foot against her opposite knee, and turned a lazy cartwheel, the Beastie backed off, watching her from a thicket of underwater ferns. Levi watched him watching.

Now the girl hung suspended in the clear water, her head above the surface, her long legs slowly scissoring. The Beastie swam up close, stretching a clawed hand out for her feet without ever quite touching her. Across the lagoon, Levi reached for both of them.

The layer of cooler water beneath him seemed tangible, something Levi could almost stand on. He hung there, feet slowly churning, as if riding a unicycle through molasses. His arms floated upward, and he held his right hand in a reverse C, as if framing a picture, and the Beastie seemed to swim right into Levi's palm.

If the cameramen turned around, trained the lens in Levi's direction, he would be captured in their machine, like an egret on the lobby wall. Would he be recognized? At this distance, would he even look human? Maybe, if only for a few seconds, they'd mistake him for some fabulous swimming creature: the legendary fish-boy of Wakulla Springs.

But the two frogmen on either side of the twin camera were focused on the latex monster and did not maneuver in his direction. Unnoticed and unbound, Levi Williams just treaded water, out of the range of capture, and after a moment's hesitation, regretfully lowered his hand, freeing the Beastie to swim on toward the girl, toward the light.

3

MONKEY BUSINESS

ISBEL WAS SO TIRED SHE COULD BARELY SIT UP. SHE'D been working on the last section of her senior thesis for two solid days, running on caffeine and Snickers bars from the vending machine. At four on a Thursday afternoon, she sat on the LaBrea bus, almost nodding off as it crawled through rush-hour traffic, jerking upright every time they hit a pothole, which in that part of Los Angeles was at least once a block.

She wished she could just call Mr. Gleckman and cancel, but the fact was, two of her studio sources had backed out at the last minute, and this was her final chance to add some really original material to bolster the library research she'd been doing since the beginning of the semester. The kind of initiative that looked good on grad school applications.

Her thesis, "An Examination of Reel vs. Real Post-Colonialism: Tarzan Movies and Imaginary Geography," was tailored to her double major in Film and the newly established Ethnic Studies department at UCLA. It was the culmination of months of work—and years of day-dreaming.

Saginaw, Michigan, her hometown, was not the sort of place anyone made a movie about. Her parents had both worked the day shift at the GM plant, so she'd been on her own after school. Her only babysitter was a man named Captain Muddy, who hosted two hours of old black-and-white movies on the local TV station. Isbel watched them all—the Three Stooges, Lash LaRue and his bullwhip, parades of stiff-legged men in monster and robot suits—but she fell completely under the spell of Tarzan the first time she saw him swing through the trees. She wanted nothing more than to escape her small gray city for the paradise of the jungle and the mysterious escarpment beyond which always lay treasure.

After two years at Michigan State, she had transferred to UCLA, and was thrilled to discover that the films' principals were still alive. She'd been trying for more than a year to get an interview—on the phone, in person, she didn't care. She'd written to the publicity departments at MGM and RKO and gotten form letters in return. She sent off queries to Johnny Weissmuller's agent, but he never replied. Maureen O'Sullivan's agent hung up on her when she called. Johnny Sheffield no longer needed an agent, and two weeks ago she'd actually managed to talk to *him* directly—at least for the thirty seconds it took for him to tell her to buzz off.

Isbel had a transcription of that phone conversation. It consisted entirely, on the part of the no-longer boyish "Boy," of : *Hello? Yes, that's me.* and *You've got to be kidding. Not a chance.* She doubted that was even enough for a footnote, much less the highlight of her paper.

Cheeta was all she had left.

At least Mr. Gleckman claimed his chimp was Cheeta. "Sure, he's the real deal. Did all the Tarzan movies," he'd said, on the phone. "In the first two, he was just the other ape's understudy, but they promoted him for *Tarzan Escapes*. That was 1936, and he's worked steady ever since. Weissmuller, Bela Lugosi, Ed Wynn—all the biggies." It sounded like a sales pitch, composed and rehearsed, but Isbel was desperate.

"You want an interview?" Mr. Gleckman had asked after ten minutes of reciting the monkey's credentials.

"Yes, please."

"He's a performer, no free shows. A hundred bucks?"

"I can get it," Isbel said. She'd hung up the phone before she could be sensible and change her mind, then gone to the bank, gutting her account, leaving just enough for groceries—if she ate mac and cheese until Thanksgiving.

The bus lumbered north on Sepulveda as Isbel fingered the five bills in the pocket of her jeans and shifted the knapsack on her knees. The snoring fat man next to her flopped a meaty arm in her direction. Draped across his lap was a copy of the *Times*. POLICE: LABIANCA, TATE SLAYINGS UNRELATED. Oh, that's reassuring, Isbel thought. Two *different* maniacs roaming the city. She sighed, watched the fast-food landscape slide past, and stroked the fringe of her purple buckskin vest, a nervous habit she was trying to break.

The address Mr. Gleckman had given her was right on the border of Encino and Tarzana, which seemed almost prophetic. She alighted with a wobble, her right leg all pins and needles, and looked at the piece of paper where she'd scribbled the address. 807-C Ventura Blvd. She looked up and down the street, seeing nothing but gas stations and vacant lots, then noticed a sign for Shady Glen Mobile Home Estates half a block down.

A trailer park? Really? Cheeta was a movie star. All right, it was a long time ago, and he was a chimp, but still. Maybe he'd spent his savings on bananas. Isbel laughed out loud, hearing the giddiness of exhaustion, and wanted nothing more than to go back to her dorm, crawl under the covers, and sleep for a week. This was a terrible idea. What had she been thinking?

She headed toward the sign.

Beyond a peeling stucco arch she saw rows and rows of neatly identical aluminum-sided trailers. Fifty feet to her right was a fenced-in, open-air pool. A very tan muscular guy in T-shirt and sweats was sifting blue crystals into the water amid a swirl of orange hoses, a panel truck backed up to the pool gate. The guy looked up and nodded.

Isbel took a few steps toward him and cupped her hands around her mouth. "Hey, do you know how I find number 807?"

"Those are the 500s." He pointed to her left. "The 800s are three rows over."

"Thanks." She turned and peered at the oversized house numbers, which seemed to go in and out of focus. She blinked, rubbing her eyes, and wished she'd at least gotten another cup of coffee before she got on the bus. Too late now. She found 807-C and stepped onto the astroturfed porch of a trailer with a wrought-iron sign that said GLECKMAN. She rang the bell, and chimes echoed inside, playing a tinny version of "Hooray for Hollywood."

The door was opened by a homely little man with a salt-and-pepper mustache and a spectacularly unconvincing dark brown toupee. It looked like a cutout from a set of bad paper dolls.

"Mr. Gleckman?"

"I got all the Watchtowers I need," he said. "And I'm down to one good crap a week, so whatever it is you're selling, it's not going to help." He started to shut the door.

"I'm Isbel Hartsoe. From UCLA? We spoke on the phone about an interview?" He was so short she was eye-to-eye with him, and she was only five-three, even in her clogs.

He took his hand off the doorknob. "Oh, yeah. How about that? You actually showed up. You're a credit to your generation," he said, reaching out and damply shaking her hand. "Call me Mort. I'm only Mr. Gleckman to the landlord and the IRS." He opened the door wider. "I guess I didn't recognize you. You sounded white on the phone."

Isbel stopped halfway across the threshold. "Excuse me?"

"Hey, hey. I got nothing against Negroes. Negroes, Jews, we're in this shit together, right? Someone told me once I sounded Irish on the phone. Me, Irish! Must have been back when I was drinking."

"I'm Cuban-American, Mr. Gleckman."

"Mort, please. So, you from Miami?"

"Michigan." Isbel took a deep breath. "May I come in?"

"Sure, sure. You got the, uh, interview fee?"

Isbel ignored the voice in her head that told her that none of this was looking promising, and pulled the folded bills from her pocket. Mort riffled them with a tobacco-stained thumb and nodded his head before inserting them into a battered wallet.

"That doesn't seem very professional," Isbel said, as he led her into a narrow hallway, "charging for an interview."

He looked genuinely surprised. "Sweetheart, that's what *pro-fessional* means," he said. "If no money changes hands, it's just amateur night." He slid a flimsy door open and gestured her inside. "And Cheeta's been a pro since before you were born."

Isbel stepped into an oppressively over-cluttered room about twelve feet square. Heavy dark furniture covered a poison-green shag rug that smelled like smoke and wet dog and a faintly acrid odor she didn't want to think about. The walls were striped with sunlight from the Venetian blinds, and encrusted with framed black-and-white photos: Men in cowboy hats. Tuxedoed saxophonists. Women wearing piles of fruit. The thermostat was cranked up high.

"The living room suite was my mother's," Mort said, following her glance. "Quality stuff." He thumped the back of a chintz-covered armchair. "Let me move those." The chair, the coffee table, the couch—every horizontal surface—was stacked with paint-spattered canvases. He cleared off the armchair, regarded the purple-and-orange stained upholstery, and covered it with a folded newspaper. "There. Sit."

Isbel noticed a spattered easel. "Do you paint?" she asked, lowering herself gingerly onto the paper.

"Nah. It's all Cheeta's."

"What?"

"Yeah, he's a regular Picasso. But cheaper. Only a hundred bucks a picture. Two for one-fifty. You know Tony Curtis? He bought five. I could give you a student discount maybe?"

"I don't think—"

"We'll talk later." Mort turned and whistled, three sharp notes.

A series of panting hoots issued from behind another sliding door on the far side of the room, and then Cheeta appeared.

Isbel's mouth opened in surprise. Chimps looked so small and cute on television, but this thing was grizzled and leathery and almost as big as she was. Cheeta's face was whiskered and gray, and he was dressed just like Mort—white shirt, suspenders, brown pants pulled up to mid-chest—with the addition of a purple beret worn at a rakish angle. He held a palette in one hand, a brush in the other. He stopped, his large brown eyes regarding her with keen disinterest, like an old roué in a Paris bar, then hooted again.

"Isbel, meet Cheeta," Mort said. "Cheeta, meet Isbel."

The chimp curled his lips back, revealing huge yellow teeth. He pointed at Mort and hooted louder.

"Yes, I know. Cocktail time. Hold your horses. We've got company." Mort turned to Isbel. "Excuse me for just a moment." He stepped over to a side table and poured a squat glass full of what looked like whiskey.

Isbel stared.

"Oh, don't worry," Mort said. "It's not for me. I've been on the wagon for years. But the big fella got a taste for Jim Beam, back in the day, and if he doesn't get his afternoon nip, well, let's just say things can get ugly." He put the glass down next to Cheeta's easel and produced a cigar from his vest pocket, lighting it with a flourish.

"I hope *that's* for you," Isbel said, although the idea of smoke added to the warm miasma of the room made her stomach knot.

"What can I say? Actors, they're not exactly known for clean living." Mort handed the cigar to the chimp, who switched the paintbrush to his bare right foot, took a long sloppy puff, and farted.

"And a good day to you, too," Mort replied. He and Cheeta both laughed loudly, Mort holding his stomach, the chimp hooting and flailing his hands. A gob of green pigment hit the lampshade and clung there. Mort fanned the air and made a face. "You get used to it. He's mostly vegetarian. All that roughage. And he's old, what can I say? Don't write that part down."

Isbel looked at her notepad and pen, unaware that she had pulled them out of her knapsack. "All right." She turned to a blank page and cleared her throat, getting down to business. "So, Mr. Gleckman. How did you—"

The phone rang in the next room. Cheeta hooted twice and flopped into a swivel chair, crossing his over-long arms over his chest.

"Yes, I know. It's my turn," Mort said, crossing to the door. He looked back at Isbel. "Hold that thought."

Half of Mort's baggy khaki backside was still visible as he picked up the receiver and shouted into the phone, "Hermie! You bastard! You got some nerve, calling me. Fuck me or pay me. What? No. Have I seen a check? Is it the arthritis? You can't hold a pen anymore? Just a sec."

His toupeed head peeked around the doorframe. "Sorry, sweetheart, but I got business. It'll only be a few minutes."

"Wait. What about my interview?" asked Isbel, both alarmed and insulted.

Mort shrugged. "Cheeta's the one you came to see, right? So talk to him. Don't worry. He likes company. Just don't make any loud noises." He disappeared behind a sliding accordion door made of wood-grained plastic. "Hermie? Yeah, I'm back. What? How much? I am hanging up this phone. Ah, okay. Now that's a number grown men can discuss. That shit you said before, I am like a dog. I cannot hear numbers that low. They are below my fucking threshold. So tell me news!" Mort pulled the door shut.

Isbel heard the flimsy plastic latch with a sucking sound, that felt like God had pressed down a Tupperware lid sealing off the cluttered, smelly room from the rest of the world, leaving her alone with Cheeta.

The chimp eyed her over the rim of his glass, as if daring her to make the first move. Isbel thought of all the questions she had prepared, all that work. She slumped into her chair with a sigh that bordered precariously on tears. If Mr. Gleckman wasn't off the phone in *two* minutes, she would ask—no, demand—the "fee" back and would leave. This was beyond ridiculous.

She watched Cheeta take another puff on his cigar, then lay it in an ashtray and move the paintbrush from foot to hand again. She wrote *Hand? Paw?* in her notebook and felt a headache coming on. The chimp slathered blue paint onto the canvas, plucked something off his cheek, gazed at it, and put it in his mouth.

"Oh, great," she said. "Movie star cooties. What's next?" She closed her eyes against the throb in her temples and sank into the soft chintz. "Some interview."

"You haven't asked any questions yet."

The gravelly voice sounded far away and muffled, but seemed to be coming from the direction of the easel.

"You might ask, for example," the voice continued, "about my experiences in show business. Because Mort knows nothing. He wasn't there, wasn't part of the magic. And I was, although you'd never know it from the posters. The jungle man, his woman, his child. Where's his best friend? I got no respect from those Hollywood types. Day after day, I watched those overpriced actors play-acting as heroes, but who was it that always saved the day, driving out the invaders, seeing through their schemes, thwarting their greed? Cheeta! But they never wrote a single line for me. When I was paid at all, it was as if I was one of the extras, some local yokel hired to be a native for a day. And I *was* from Africa! But here's how good an actor I was. I warned my friends without words, playacting on my own, hooting and miming as if I really was a creature of the dark jungles and the swamps. And I *saved* them. Saved Tarzan, Jane, Boy, the whole lot of them. But more importantly, kid—I saved the picture. I was the one who got the laughs. I was the one the audience came to see. And what happens? Weissmuller gets two grand a week and I get bananas and a scritch on the head as if I'm nothing but a dumb beast. But off-camera? You've read the tabloids. The humans were the ones who acted like animals. Sure, times were different then. But has anything changed? That's up to you. I'll never get the back pay I'm due, but at least you can help me set the record straight. I want my legacy. I want everyone in Hollywood—in the whole world—to remember this: I stood upright among the best of them. Cheeta was a star."

Mort slid the accordion door open. "Sorry, sweetheart. That took longer than I thought."

Isbel opened her eyes and looked around. Had she fallen asleep? It should be later than it was. But the yellow stripes of dust-filled afternoon light reached no higher up the flimsy, fussy walls than they had when she arrived.

"Well, will you look at that!" Mort said. "He did a painting of you. Ain't that something?"

On the canvas was a set of orange loops against a dark blue background, like a Hot Wheels track in the sky.

Cheeta looked at Isbel, raised a hairy eyebrow, and hooted softly.

"Sometimes, it almost seems like he can talk, doesn't it?" Mort smiled and sat on the couch. "Okay, now. Whad'ya wanna know?"

Isbel looked down at the open page of her notebook, which was completely filled with scribbles. She stared at the words *I stood upright among the best of them.*

"Sweetheart, you okay? You look, excuse me for saying it, the same color as a lime at the bottom of a Mai Tai." He peered at her. "You're not *on* something, are you?"

"No." Isbel shook her head, which throbbed with the motion. "But I'm really not feeling well. I think it would be better if I, um—rescheduled."

"Sure, sure. Anytime. Me and Cheeta, we're always here. Except Thursdays. I play pinochle on Thursdays."

"Another time, then." Isbel stood, using the arm of the chair for balance, and took a step toward the door before she remembered her money. "The—fee—Mr. Gleckman?" She held out her hand.

"Consider it an advance."

"I don't think so."

Man and chimp both stared at her for a minute. Then Mort sighed and reached for his wallet. "You sure? It might be more, next time."

"I'll take my chances." Isbel returned the bills to the pocket of her jeans.

Outside, walking through the array of aluminum housing,

Isbel felt on the verge of what she was afraid might be hysteria. Not only had she hallucinated a soliloquy by a chimpanzee, she had taken notes. With a shudder, she shoved the notebook deep inside her knapsack. She'd read whatever was in it tomorrow, after she'd had some sleep. A lot of sleep. Then she'd probably burn it.

She mustered a smile and a nod for a not-so-young woman in Capri pants who walked past, giving her an odd look. Was she talking out loud, too? Isbel bit her lip and walked with careful attention, footstep by footstep, her shoulders pageant-perfect, as if she could will herself to remain upright long enough to get to the bus. But when she reached the pool and spotted a deck chair, a comfortable-looking arrangement of blue-and-white plastic mesh, a few minutes' rest seemed like an excellent idea. The bus stop was still a block away.

The pool guy's hoses had been rolled into neat coils, and he was in the water, doing laps with long, easy strokes. He looked like he was half fish, a dark streak gliding just under the surface, only coming up for air once in two lengths. Isbel flopped down onto the deck chair as if her bones had turned to Jell-O.

A few minutes later, she felt a coolness as something blocked the sun.

"Are you okay?" the pool guy asked. He had a bit of a southern-sounding drawl.

"A little tired," she replied sleepily. "Other than that, I'm just peachy. How about you?"

"Right as rain." She heard the sound of feet shuffling, the clink of an aluminum pole on concrete. The man cleared his throat. "Ma'am? You sure you're okay?"

Ma'am? With enormous effort, Isbel opened her eyes. Jesus, he was gorgeous, copper-cocoa skin and a smoothly muscled body as sleek and lithe as an animal's, poured into a pair of blue Speedos. She looked down at the ground so she wouldn't stare and swung her feet to the concrete. "Sorry. I'm fine. I pulled a couple of all-nighters, that's all."

"Ah." He put on a pair of sweat pants, then picked up a skimmer pole and dismantled it into three sections, laying it down by a jug of chlorine. "You're in school?"

"UCLA."

"Encino's a long drive. What brings you to Shady Glen?"

"I had an interview with a movie star." She thought of her note-book, filled with the sage musings of Tarzan's simian sidekick.

He looked around. "Somebody famous lives *here*?"

"I thought so, but it didn't work out quite like I expected." She shook her head—which had stopped throbbing quite so much once she got out into fresh air—and changed the subject. "You're a hell of a swimmer."

"Thanks." He busied himself with the screw-top for the gallon jug.

"Do you compete?"

"Not really. After high school I was hoping to go pro—stunt work for the movies. That's why I moved out here." He tugged on his t-shirt.

"What happened?"

"Turns out there aren't many swimming movies these days, and even if there were, not a lot of brothers in them, know what I mean? So I got a job lifeguarding at the Y, started learning about the pool equipment and filters and such. It was all new to me. Back home in Florida, I just swam in the river, or the springs, or the sink."

Isbel laughed. "You must have been pretty little, to swim in a sink."

"Not that kind. A sinkhole. Natural limestone formation. Lots a'those where I'm from. You might have heard of it. Wakulla Springs? They filmed a couple of movies there."

"Really? Which ones?" Isbel sat up straighter.

"*Creature from the Black Lagoon?*" He looked at her as if hoping for some reaction, then shrugged. "And a couple of the Tarzans, back before I was born."

"*Weissmuller* Tarzans?"

"Yep. You should hear my Aunt Vergie go on about the mischief that man got up to. Lots of stories."

"Do you remember any of them?"

"Bits and pieces."

"Could I interview *you*?" Suddenly Isbel wasn't as tired.

He smiled. "I don't know if I've got much worth telling, but sure." He looked down at the equipment by his feet. "Let me get all this back into the truck, and I'll give you a ride home." He picked up a bucket stenciled *Wakulla Joe's Pools.* "The office is in Santa Monica, so it's almost on the way."

She looked at him and shook her head. "Thanks, but—"

"But I'm a total stranger?" He smiled. "Don't worry, I didn't kill Sharon Tate or anything. And I'm not just the pool guy. I'm the owner. Stand-up citizen. I got five crews working all over LA. I'm usually in the office, but Carl had Guard duty this week." He shook his head. "Lord knows where Governor Reagan might send him. Here." He dug through his toolbox and handed her a wicked-looking long-handled trowel with a narrow blade.

"What's that for?"

"Well, I use it to dig moss out of cracks in pools, but you have my permission to run me through like a gigged frog if you feel threatened anywhere between here and Westwood. Okay?"

"I guess." Isbel still wasn't sure, but the lure of *truly* original material—unpublished, never-before-heard Tarzan stories!—was too much to resist.

"Great." He smiled. "Then allow me to introduce myself proper. I'm Levi Williams."

"Isbel Hartsoe." She hefted the tool and smiled back. "You're taking a big risk. Suppose *I'm* a killer on the loose?"

"Well," Levi said, "then I reckon I'm just shit out of luck. But my mama's got a custom for just about every kind of luck there is, and she gave me one of her Indian head pennies to watch over my van, so I reckon I'll be safe." He picked up a coil of hose.

"Do you believe everything your Mama tells you?"

He chuckled. "Not by half. But she did raise me to have respect for the traditions other folks hold store in."

"Your mama sounds a lot like my *abuela*. My grandmother. She's from Cuba. Lots of superstitions." Isbel picked up her knapsack. "I think most of them are tall tales, but then there are days . . . " Her voice trailed off as she thought again about the scribbles in her notebook.

"I hear you." Levi laughed. "I was raised in *Florida*, and let me tell you, I've spent so much time on the river, in the woods, in the swamps—hell, I believe in *everything*."

4

WATERS OF
MYSTERY

PADDLING SLOWLY DOWN THE WAKULLA RIVER FELT like coming home for Dr. Anna Williams. Although she had grown up in Southern California, her family had alternated holidays—spending Christmas one year with Abuela Cecelia in Michigan, the next with Granny Mayola in Florida. And although she adored both her grandmothers, she always felt like she belonged here. Saginaw just couldn't hold a candle to the natural wonders of the springs.

On a hot, humid August afternoon she sat motionless in the bow of her fifteen-foot jon boat, a catch-pole at the ready in her double-gloved right hand, a hook in her left. Her paddle lay athwart the second bench, dripping into the flat bottom, unneeded. The lazy current drew the boat forward as easily and quietly as that azalea blossom spiraling past, toward the island.

She scanned the vegetation, and caught her breath. Trouble. *Possible* trouble, she reminded herself. The snake coiled amid the palmetto thicket might be a native. She couldn't discern the patterning from this distance; only a forearm's length of brown-and-tan scales was visible through the sawblade leaves. So instead of steering around the island as she had umpteen times before, Anna eased bow-first into the surrounding hydrilla fronds, which hissed along the aluminum hull as the boat's snub nose thumped ashore.

The snake didn't budge until Anna prodded it with the hook. Then it flexed like a strongman's arm and threw itself to the left, but Anna's reflexes were just as quick. She tightened the noose of the catchpole around its head, planted her feet squarely in the bilge of the forgiving flat-hulled boat, and lifted the writhing creature free of the vegetation.

Almost four feet, she estimated, and unusually thick. Possibly a pregnant female. She eased it up a few more inches and saw that the scale pattern was clearly a checkerboard. Just a brown water snake. Her students would laugh if they'd seen her. Professor Williams mistaking a common water snake for a Burmese python?

She released the annoyed reptile and sighed with relief. Although it would have been exciting to be the wildlife biologist who bagged the Panhandle's first confirmed python—more than 400 miles north of the Everglades, their documented adopted habitat—it would have been very bad news for *this* environment.

Anna swished the pole through the water to remove any scales, and looked around at a landscape that had not changed much in thousands of years. It was a state park now, protected from development, and past the hotel and the springs, there was almost no sign of human habitation. But she knew that civilization was closing in. It was why she was here, spending her sabbatical documenting the changes, hoping she could find a way to turn back time.

Divers had explored the limestone caves beneath the springs, discovering more than fifteen miles of branching channels that ran unseen beneath pavement and pastures, all the way to the Apalachicola National Forest. The aquifer was being tainted by wastewater from Tallahassee and nitrate fertilizers from farmlands, turning stretches of the formerly crystal-clear waters as dark as iced tea. It was on its way to becoming a real black lagoon.

She was just as worried about the creatures that had invaded her childhood playground. Florida was home to more non-native species than anywhere else, the promised land for escapees: the hydrilla weed that choked off the surface, introduced as an aquarium decoration; pythons, boas, and anacondas brought up from South America and set free from amusement parks and tiny zoos; armadillos released from monkey jungles; and countless more former pets left behind by tourists since the 1920s.

It was still the most amazing place Anna had ever seen.

She plucked a fistful of beautyberries—a natural mosquito repellent—crushed them and rubbed the lavender juice into her forearms and neck and face. She pushed away from the island, wiping the sweat from her forehead with a bandana. She'd survey for another hour, then head back to the springs for a swim, work off a day of sitting and paddling. She was an excellent swimmer with her share of collegiate trophies, but she couldn't hold a candle to her dad. Levi Williams must have been born in the water; even at seventy he could hold his breath a full minute longer than she could.

She picked up the paddle and steered the boat past the gentle curve where Dad used to point out Old Joe basking in the sun—before a poacher downgraded the huge gator from a riverbank guardian to a relic in a glass display case in the lobby of the Lodge—and nosed into a trio of mangrove knees. She slipped her sweaty hands out of the gloves, waving them in the air to dry before she took her tablet out of the waterproof rucksack, opened the database app and added the water snake to the afternoon's tally of gators, tortoises, pelicans, anhingas, herons, and ibises. She was glad that the Wildlife Commission had given her an intern to count fish.

Anna had been happy when the Commission invited her to join the Wakulla research project. It gave her an excuse to spend one more summer at her grandmother's little house in Shadeville. At 86, Granny was a tough old bird who sat on her porch from sun-up to sundown drinking lemonade and waiting for the Bookmobile. She said she didn't need any looking after, but Anna knew she was glad to have the company.

And the project also gave her the possibility for furthering an ambition of her own. Officially, she was making a count of the wildlife whose habitat was the two-and-a-half miles of the Wakulla River between its origin at the springs and the chain-link fence that marked the boundary of the state park. Unofficially, she was hoping to sight some creatures that didn't exist, at least not any more—a black panther, a Carolina parakeet, or an ivory-billed woodpecker. Maybe even a Skunk Ape.

Common sense and professional dignity dictated that she keep her cryptozoological tendencies to herself. But Anna had been raised on the combination of tall tales and midnight monster movies that so delighted her father. He took her and her brothers on field trips to the La Brea Tar Pits, bought them Ben Cooper monster masks for Halloween, and lulled them to an uneasy sleep with stories about the swamp creatures of his own childhood. Every time she'd visited Granny, Anna had laid awake listening to every cypress branch scraping the tin roof at night, sure it was a Skunk Ape trying to peel the house open like a can. Part of her was terrified, but another part had always been thrilled by the idea that some of the tales *could* be true. She cherished discoveries like the coelacanth and the Javan elephant, and hoped one day to add to that list. Not myth. Not extinct. Here's proof.

She swatted at a swarm of no-see-ums, bringing her attention back to the task she was being paid for. She counted five more tortoises, eight gulls, a really big water strider—that made her paddle faster because she did have a few issues with Florida's insects—a nice ten-foot alligator, and—

Bloomp!

Something splashed to her right. She looked up into a cloudless sky. Nothing could have dropped from an overhead branch; she was in the middle of the river.

Ker-chunk!

That was much closer, soaking her right arm. She looked toward the south bank and her eyes widened. Any human being who met Anna's gaze from within those interlaced fingers of foliage would have caught a momentary glimpse of a scared child looking out from her adult face. But the thing watching her from the bushes wasn't human, though it had alert and intelligent eyes, a long pink face, and a grayish-brown beard. It smiled with a toothy grimace.

Anna's pulse slowed when she recognized a rhesus monkey, which cocked a skinny arm, and let fly another rock. That one plunked into the river well short of the boat. Anna laughed as the monkey screeched, inspiring a derisive chorus. There were others back there—many others—but all less brave, merely egging on their leader.

The monkeys were invaders, too, but Anna founded them harder to dislike than pythons. Cuter, more anthropomorphic. And they didn't eat all the other animals. Urban legend claimed they were descended from Hollywood monkeys, released into the wild when a Tarzan movie wrapped. Anna was skeptical; she had watched all those jungle flicks—her parents owned both the Weissmuller DVD sets—and had noticed capuchins and spider monkeys, but no rhesus macaques. That didn't mean it wasn't possible. Maybe their ancestors had just ended up on the cutting room floor. All Anna knew was that monkeys were not native to Florida, so *some*one must have let them loose, back in the day.

The lead monkey screeched again. Anna smiled and took out her phone, snapping a picture with the zoom function to get a nice close-up of the face. No cell reception out here, but when she got back to the Lodge, she'd email it to her mom with a note, "Any interview questions for this one?"—a reference to her parents' oft-told, so-cute, how-we-met story. Then she switched from smartass daughter to dutiful biologist and added three monkeys to the database, using an asterisk, because she'd *heard* at least a dozen more, even if she hadn't actually seen them.

She was almost to the moss-draped chain-link fence that was the downstream border of Edward Ball Wakulla Springs State Park. Beyond lay the Shadetown Road bridge, and the intrusion of the twenty-first century: a series of subdivisions with street names like Limpkin Court and Turkey Trail and Razorback Road, all named for whatever had been killed or displaced to build them.

The fence marked the end of paradise. It was time to turn back, call it a day.

But seeing the monkeys, thinking about where they'd come from—and where *she*'d come from—had put a bee in her bonnet, as Granny would say, to do something she hadn't done since she was a kid.

Would a noise qualify as invasive? There was decibel-based pollution, sure. But what about a sound that was artificially introduced into the landscape, only to propagate unexpectedly, crowding out the natives? Because, surely, before the 1930s, Florida children like her dad must have created their own yells of look-at-me exhilaration when they swung out on a vine and dropped into the middle of a swimming hole, right?

Anna laid down her paddle. She took a deep breath. She balled her hands into fists, raised them and beat on her chest like a drum. She opened her mouth wide and began to yell—to yodel, really, a yell more Austrian than African, more Hollywood than Florida, a fake that over time had become real.

"*Aaahhh-eeeeeee-aaahhhh-eeeee-aaaahhhh-eeeeee-aaaah-hhhh!*"

Her long, ululating cry pierced the quiet of the jungle.

It carried across the surface of the water, and the animals responded.

Two anhingas broke their cover, flapped into the cypress tops.

A family of rhesus macaques chortled and hooted and beat their own chests.

A limpkin emitted a rattling scream.

A twelve-foot gator slid into the river and lazily stroked upstream away from the din, its prehistoric brain ticking coolly away.

Anna gave the call again, queen of this jungle, primal and fearless.

Back in the trees something that smelled of sour cabbage dragged its knuckles and roared: *woomp, woomp.*

An armadillo fully as big as a VW bug shook its scaly head, snorted, and lumbered through the brush.

And beneath the river's surface, a creature reached for Anna's boat with a webbed hand, its talons approaching the metal hull. Then it changed its mind and kicked away, back down into the depths where it dwelled, away from the light.